Mrs. Pollifax
and the Golden
Triangle

Mrs. Pollifax and the Golden Triangle

Dorothy Gilman

Doubleday NEW YORK
1988

All of the characters in this book are fictitious
and any resemblance to actual persons,
living or dead, is purely coincidental.

Library of Congress Cataloging-in-Publication Data
Gilman, Dorothy, 1923–
   Mrs. Pollifax and the Golden Triangle.
   I. Title.
PS3557.I433M67   1988   813'.54   87–13082
ISBN 0-385-23710-3

All Rights Reserved
Printed in the United States of America
First Edition

This book is happily dedicated
to
Jon Butters and Jackie Johnson
&
Chris Butters and Kim Herrick

Mrs. Pollifax
and the Golden
Triangle

The village of Chiang Saen in northern Thailand lies along the Mekong River near the apex of the Golden Triangle where Laos, Burma and Thailand meet. Its main street is shadowed by palms and by a long line of thatched roofs under which shops have proliferated, and where the public commerce of the village takes place. There are guesthouses where more private transactions take place, and a restaurant where one can lunch and gaze across the broad calm Mekong, watch the occasional long-tailed boat motor up or down the river and observe the low line of trees and yellow sand on the opposite Laotian shore. There are also two *wats* for tourists to visit, if interested in the history of the area: the Wat Pa Sak, and the Wat Prathat Chom Kitto, which dates back to the tenth century when Chiang Saen was the site of a very ancient kingdom.

In one of the thatch-roofed guesthouses, on a certain afternoon in October, a man stood ransacking the desk files of an American *farang* who lay curled up on a nearby low couch. If the resident *farang* saw the intruder he gave no indication of it: his wide-open eyes were unfocused and their pupils dilated, the expression on his face intent on an interior world of fantasies and delusions. As the intruder found and read certain papers in the file he grunted, giving sidelong glances at the man on the couch, and then he very carefully replaced the papers. Only one of them captured his attention to the end; it held an address that he copied in pencil on a slip of crumpled paper, forming the letters with care.

Walking noiselessly across the room he helped himself to a pen, an envelope, a handful of Thai stamps and a sheet of writing paper before he left the house, closing the door quietly behind him. Presently, seated comfortably under a tree by the river he copied out the address on the long white envelope. It read:

> Mr. James T. Carstairs,
> P. O. Box 4023,
> Baltimore, Maryland, USA

Nibbling thoughtfully at the tip of the pen he began to write his message on the sheet of paper. When he had finished—it was a long message—he took out a pad of ink, rubbed his thumb across it and added his fingerprint to the note, which he signed in block letters RUAMSAK.

With the letter stamped and sealed he held it for a moment in his hand as if testing its weight, but actually he was weighing the arduous path that he was about to take: to post a letter to the United States in Chiang Saen would be dangerous, inviting comment and attention, which meant that he would have to drive to Mae Sai or even as far as Chiang Rai to post it, and then he would have to frequently check the receiving address as well. He sighed as he reflected on how very inconvenient all this was going to be for a busy man, but his sigh was followed by a shrug; he had already learned what kind of money was being paid for information and he had asked himself why others should be paid for what he knew. He would insist on being paid in gold, and to propitiate the *phi*-spirits he would give a little money to the monks and take a garland of flowers to his house-shrine, *phra-phuum.*

It was decided. It would be done.

Tucking the letter into his belt he rose and set out for Mae Sai to mail his letter to a distant Baltimore. It would be postmarked October 17, and he thought the information he was sending would please the Americans very much and assure him of a reply.

Chapter 1

Sunshine poured like melted butter across oak floors; ice melting from the roof produced rhythmic and musical *pings!* on the terrace outside. It was January, and Mrs. Pollifax, list in hand, looked doubtfully at the pair of suitcases standing by the front door and said, "Are you quite sure we've not forgotten something?"

Cyrus Reed said dryly, "Emily, you've gone over that list four times this morning. Between my legal mind and your imaginative one, how could anything have been overlooked?"

"It's the imaginative half that worries me," she told him frankly. "I know I packed your precious survival food—those six tins of sardines—but now I'm wondering if I packed my malaria tablets, and if so, where?"

Cyrus replied by grasping her by the shoulders and steering her into the kitchen. "Breakfast, Emily," he said firmly. "Scrambled eggs are waiting. My God, Emily, after all the traveling you've done—"

She smiled up at him sunnily, an act that required a major tilt of the head because Cyrus was well over six feet tall. "Traveling yes," she reminded him, "but you know I've never been a real tourist before. Only a pretend one for Carstairs and the Department."

"Yes I know," he said, amused. "Getting bashed over the head by an assassin in Zambia—"

"Well, I'd never have met you if—"

"—not to mention sniffing out the KGB in China."

She noticed that very wisely he was not including her last adventure, when the odds had caught up with her and she had endured the nearly worst that could happen. "Well, it does seem strange," she mused, taking her place at the table. "A real holiday, not a care in the world . . . Delicious eggs," she told him, fork in hand. "What did you put in them this morning?"

"Garlic, parsley and a pinch of salt," he said, pouring coffee.

"I'll try to remember that when it's my turn. Do you suppose I tucked the malaria tablets in with the vitamins, Cyrus? We leave in four hours," she reminded him.

He smiled and lifted his glass of orange juice. "To Thailand, m'dear—and to malaria tablets *definitely* packed with your vitamins."

"Good," she said, and nodded happily, still very aware that she'd nearly lost all this, as well as her life, in Hong Kong a few months ago, and grateful that she could still look at Cyrus across the breakfast table each morning, at his thatch of white hair, the broad shoulders, his sleepy smile and the eyes set so oddly in his face that he resembled a Chinese mandarin. "To temple bells and dancing girls and elephants," she said, touching her glass to his, and then as the doorbell stridently rang she put down her glass and sighed. "Now who on earth can that be at ten o'clock on a Sunday morning!"

"Only one way to find out," Cyrus told her.

"I'll go—you made breakfast," she said, and pushed back her chair and hurried into the living room, annoyed that whoever was ringing their doorbell seemed determined to continue until acknowledged. Circumnavigating the suitcases she opened the door and drew in her breath sharply: an attractive sandy-haired man in a sheepskin jacket stood beaming at her, attaché case in hand.

"Thank God you're still here," he said, and removed his finger from the doorbell.

"Bishop?" she faltered. *"Bishop?"*

Cyrus, following her to the door, said doubtfully, "Bishop? Met you last June, didn't I? Bishop, isn't it?"

"I seem to have trouble establishing my identity this morning," said Bishop cheerfully. "You're making me feel like an apparition from the spirit world but I'm quite alive, thank you, although in danger of freezing to death standing here. May I come in?"

"Coffee," said Mrs. Pollifax, nodding. "Come in at *once,* Bishop, although you must admit—" Abandoning her sentence she led him into the living room and divested him of his coat, her mind already racing with thoughts of what his appearance meant, because Bishop was assistant to Carstairs of the CIA, and although she and Bishop were excellent friends they never met face to face without its signaling a new adventure.

Except what an inopportune moment, she thought, when they were leaving in less than four hours for the airport and their flight to Bangkok; they would have to refuse him, of course, any change being absolutely impossible when she and Cyrus had spent so many weeks planning this holiday.

"No eggs left," Cyrus told him. "Settle for half a Danish and coffee?"

"The gods are smiling," said Bishop, following him into the kitchen and rubbing his hands together. "Oh—handsome," he said, glancing around appreciatively. "Lots of sunshine."

"Sit and revive," Mrs. Pollifax told him, coffeepot in hand.

Cyrus presented him with what remained of a large Danish pastry and sat down facing him. He said bluntly, "Should tell you we're leaving on holiday in four hours."

Bishop, crumbs dropping all around him, smiled and nodded his head. "So Emily bed," he said, his mouth full. Swallowing, he took a sip of coffee and leaned back in his chair. "Nothing like a transfusion of coffee, is there? I'm really getting too old for this sort of rushing around but I've caught you in time, thank Heaven, which I must say is satisfying. I had to move so fast there wasn't time to phone."

"Hard to believe," said Cyrus, looking amused.

"On the contrary I left Virginia at 3 A.M.—that's three o'clock in the *morning,"* he emphasized. "Enough to infect anyone with martyrdom."

He didn't look martyred, thought Mrs. Pollifax, nor did he look at all old from rushing about; he was wearing a shirt open at the neck and a soft blue sweater over it, and he looked astonishingly boyish in spite of the frenetic life he lived as Carstairs' aide and the years that she'd known him. "What," she asked, "has produced this wild urge to have coffee with us?"

"Thailand," he said.

Mrs. Pollifax stared at him blankly. "Did I mention it to you?"

"Of course—in your Christmas note. 'P.S.,' you wrote, 'Cyrus and I are off to Thailand January 12th, and for nothing but a holiday, isn't that amazing?' "

Cyrus said dryly, "I take it no longer?" Despite his cryptic manner of talking and his sleepy eyes the air of laziness that he exuded was totally deceptive; Mrs. Pollifax knew that he was already probing Bishop's psyche adroitly and shrewdly.

Bishop smiled disarmingly. "Well—here you are, all packed and ready to go, which is too splendid a coincidence to be overlooked when we need a pair of Innocent Tourists for Thailand in a hurry—in fact needed them practically yesterday. Damn providential, actually." He added politely, "Just where do you plan to go first?"

"We intend to browse," Mrs. Pollifax told him. "A few days in Bangkok and then we'll fly to Sukotai—the old kingdom, you know—and inspect all the temples, and then go on to Chiang Mai . . . I understand that venturing farther north isn't safe yet for tourists."

Bishop put down his cup of coffee and shook his head. "Now there you're wrong, you must have an out-of-date guidebook. It's perfectly safe now in the north so long as you don't wander off the beaten paths. The area's been opened up in the past few years, thanks to a road built clear up to the Laotian and Burmese borders. It's no longer isolated: schools are being built, the border patrol's active . . . All beside the point, however, because all we'd ask, if you could slightly rearrange—"

"Still opium?" interrupted Cyrus.

"Opium?" Bishop said blankly. "Oh, the Golden Triangle, and all that. Well, of course opium's not easily eradicated when the hill tribes in the north have grown it for generations but things are changing, you know. The King's been active in that, researching and promoting substitute crops—coffee, tobacco, that sort of thing—and there's a limit now on how many acres of poppies the hill tribes can plant for their own use. And then of course—as you've probably read—the United States subsidizes raids on the poppy fields when any of them get out of hand." He shrugged. "Of course a lot of the stuff still comes into the country from Burma so no one can say there's not still a problem but that needn't concern you. If you could rearrange your—"

Mrs. Pollifax, having done her homework, nodded wisely. "The Shans."

"I beg your pardon?"

"The Shans in Burma, just over the mountains, the ones still rebelling against joining the union of Burma."

"You do seem informed," he said appreciatively. "Yes, they're pretty much the culprits where drug smuggling's concerned—still wanting an autonomous state and to be independent of Burma, and of course the only way they can buy weapons to fight their war is to sell their opium for guns."

"In Thailand," contributed Cyrus.

"Yes, but this has nothing to do with—look, it's Chiang Mai we hope you can get to as quickly as possible," he explained, "and Chiang Mai, I can assure you, is nearly a hundred miles from the Golden Triangle. Could you—*would* you—consider rearranging your itinerary by going to Chiang Mai first? On a very *small* errand," he added.

Cyrus chuckled. "So small you've come all the way from Virginia on a Sunday morning?"

"Small for you, important for us," Bishop told him brightly. "Strictly a matter of picking up a packet of information on Thursday morning from a chap in Chiang Mai named Ruamsak."

"How on earth do you spell *that?*" asked Mrs. Pollifax.

Bishop spelled it for her. "Very mysterious chap, we don't know a thing about him except that twice he's sent us surprisingly valuable and accurate information."

Cyrus, regarding Bishop steadily, said, "Not sure that Emily—after the Hong Kong misadventure—ought to tackle anything for you so soon. Just getting over it, you know. This trip—pure holiday—is actually to—"

Bishop's face sobered as he turned to Mrs. Pollifax. "Still nightmares?"

She shook her head. "Not now, no." She smiled. "Cyrus recommended some wonderful therapy for me, I've been taking lessons in magic from a retired magician."

Bishop whistled. "Good heavens! Karate, yoga and now magic . . . Have you sawed anyone in half yet?"

She grinned. "No but I'm growing rather clever at palming coins."

He nodded. "Okay, you no longer have nightmares and you can palm coins but how is your back?"

"Healing."

Bishop looked at Cyrus and then at her and shook his head. "I must be losing my grip but I suddenly realize I can't push this Chiang Mai errand no matter *how* uncomplicated it is. The Department can be quite ruthless, you know, but damn it I can't. If you're still recovering from Hong Kong I'll cease and desist and leave quietly."

Mrs. Pollifax considered this thoughtfully. "On the other hand," she said softly, and hesitated. "On the other hand don't they say that when a person has fallen off a horse the best prescription is to climb back on the horse at once? If it's just a small errand—"

Cyrus said, "It wasn't a horse you fell off, Emily."

"No," she admitted, "but—is that all? Just collect a small package?"

Bishop nodded. "That's all."

In the silence that followed Cyrus said pleasantly, "Isn't your department already well represented in Thailand, what with the country providing air bases for the United States during the Vietnam War, and it being friend and ally, bastion of freedom and all that?"

"Well—it's all a bit tricky," Bishop said cautiously. "Actually we're not that popular anymore. At their insistence we pulled out of Thailand in 1976—removed our radar listening posts, our planes, soldiers, et cetera and they at once began signing friendship pacts with China, Laos, Cambodia—or Kampuchea as it's called now. You might say for survival, because—well, just look at any map: to the west lies Burma, their traditional, centuries-old enemy—Burma in the old days plundered and occupied Thailand—and to the north lies China, which in 1976 was supplying Thai insurgents in the north with weapons at the same time it was signing that friendship pact with the Thai government in Bangkok. To the northeast is Laos, now taken over by Hanoi, while on their eastern border lies Cambodia—sorry, Kampuchea —into which the Vietnamese have moved, precipitating certain hells along that border, as you know, and a flood of refugees.

"Thailand is thus surrounded. Presumably the government at some point decided they couldn't fully trust us to protect them, in spite of our having a number of treaties with them, so they opted for the ASEAN and their own resources." He sighed. "I might add that Thailand keeps reaching for a democracy that it can't manage yet—the army dominates the government—and this has resulted in umpteen coups in the past. The governments come and go . . . only the King and Buddhism keep things glued together . . . *so far.*

"Under such circumstances," he added with a faint smile, "we try to keep open private channels of information so we know what's going on behind the scenes. Very unofficially, of course."

"Of course," said Mrs. Pollifax dryly. "But—why us, Bishop?"

"Well, to be absolutely frank with you—"

"Yes, do be," she told him cordially.

"To be absolutely frank we don't want anyone, Thai or American, to hear about this—er—connection. Ruamsak's new, and shows signs of being too valuable an informant to risk anyone learning about him, for his sake as well as ours."

"Ah, an informer," said Mrs. Pollifax, nodding pleasantly. "Cyrus, what do you think?"

He said firmly, "Has to be up to you, m'dear. Sounds simple enough, of course. As usual," he added dryly.

"And Cyrus would be with you," Bishop added, a note of hope returning to his voice.

After a glance at his wife's face Cyrus said, "Just what is it we'd be picking up?"

"Information effectively disguised, but how we don't know. We've been told it's a very incriminating document too dangerous to mail, so it will be turned over to you disguised as some sort of tourist souvenir. We've also been told that Ruamsak can't linger for more than a few hours in Chiang Mai—it *has* to be Thursday morning."

Mrs. Pollifax thought about this. She could detect none of Bishop's usual tension when any assignment proposed to her held the possibility of danger. She decided that she believed him when he described it as a very small errand, and certainly his precipitous arrival on their doorstep implied a definite need. Looking at Cyrus she said, "I suppose we could manage that easily enough. Would you mind our mixing business with pleasure?"

Cyrus studied her face; apparently he was reassured by what he saw. "Of course I wouldn't mind. So long as you feel comfortable about it, keeping that horse analogy in mind, no problem."

Bishop drew a deep sigh of relief. "Wonderful," he said, and opened his attaché case. "Somewhere I've a map of Chiang Mai for you . . ."

Cyrus frowned. "Hearing you say Chiang Mai has been ringing bells." His frown deepened. "Didn't John Lloyd Matthews
disappear in Chiang Mai on a visit there?"

Bishop looked at him in surprise. "But that was years ago—
nearly ten years ago, surely! What a memory."

"Ah, but you see I knew him," Cyrus said mildly. "High
school days in Connecticut. Played baseball together—on the
same boxing team, too. Had a good left."

"Who on earth are we talking about?" asked Mrs. Pollifax.

"John Lloyd Matthews," explained Bishop. "U.S. diplomat in
Bangkok who disappeared some years back, rather like the famous old Judge Crater disappearance."

Because the details had been so dramatic at the time Mrs.
Pollifax found herself remembering, too. "But yes," she said eagerly, "didn't he leave a cigar burning on the terrace—and a
book open—and he'd just been brought coffee, and then minutes
later his host came back and he was gone?"

"That's the one," Bishop said, spreading out a street map of
Chiang Mai on the table.

"No trace ever?" inquired Cyrus.

Bishop shook his head. "Not a single clue. I believe the final
conclusion was that he'd been seized for ransom by insurgents or
drug people—those were rougher days in the north—and put up
a fight at some point and was killed and buried in the jungle."

"I wondered at the time if he worked for you people," Cyrus
said.

Bishop looked amused. "You're not the first person to wonder
that, it makes a great story, but I can assure you absolutely not.
He was, however, instrumental in getting Thailand the very best
of deals when we asked for air bases there—he really loved Thailand—and you'll find that your guidebook lists a couple of stat-
ues of him over there. Here we are . . ." He smoothed out the
map of Chiang Mai and they leaned closer. "I've written all the
details down but here's where you'll find Ruamsak, behind one of
the shops near the eastern gate—see Thapae Road? You'll note

the printed locations of the Night Bazaar, Wat Chang Khong, Wat Mahawan . . . see?"

They nodded.

"You'll find Thapae Road lined with shops: lacquerware, silk, cotton, et cetera . . . Between the Pekanant Silk Shop—the name's in English as well as Thai—and the Apichat Lacquerware there's a narrow alley. Duck down it, and behind the lacquerware factory there's a small abandoned house—a hut really, I suppose —with what Ruamsak describes as a wooden fence spilling over with bougainvillea. Ruamsak will be expecting to deliver his package to someone on Thursday morning between eight o'clock and twelve noon."

Cyrus grunted. "Rather conspicuous, isn't it, a pair of tourists ducking down a private alley?"

Bishop grinned. "Tourists with cameras are forgiven anything. Just be sure you have cameras."

"Yes," said Mrs. Pollifax, growing interested now, "but how will this person—this Ruamsak—know we're anything more than tourists with cameras?"

"Because you'll give him this," Bishop said, bringing out a terra-cotta object from his pocket and placing it on the table.

Mrs. Pollifax picked it up and found that it fitted neatly into the palm of her hand but with much more weight than its size implied. She held it out for Cyrus to see: an elongated oval with a primitive Buddha-image molded into its terra-cotta background.

"Buddhist votive tablet," explained Bishop. "You'll find people carrying them in Thailand for protection."

"It's certainly charming," said Mrs. Pollifax, "but isn't it rather heavy to carry around in a pocket?"

Bishop grinned. "Actually what you're holding is a cube of gold bullion with a thin veneer of terra-cotta to conceal it. Just so you know what you've got there."

"Payment?" said Cyrus.

"Partial, yes." Closing his attaché case he smiled at them. "So that's it, then. With the time change you'll arrive in Bangkok late Monday evening and I suggest you fly to Chiang Mai on Wednesday, which will give you a full day on Tuesday to recover from jet lag. We'll reserve two seats for you on the plane to Chiang Mai, and a room for you there at the Orchid Hotel. Where are you staying in Bangkok?"

"The Oriental Hotel."

"Good." He nodded. "We'll see to it that your plane tickets are delivered to you there." He stood up, bestowing a warm smile on them both. "I can't tell you what a relief it will be to not worry about you this time—two of you, after all!—not to mention your agreeing to do this for us. I wish you both a wonderful and well-deserved holiday . . . oh and by the way, we'd appreciate your phoning us from Chiang Mai on Thursday once you've met with Ruamsak—Carstairs likes to tidy up loose ends and cross things off lists and all that."

"You must remember us to him," said Mrs. Pollifax. "And how do we deliver this package to you?"

"At the moment," said Bishop crisply, "our principle concern —of the utmost importance—is to collect the package before Ruamsak vanishes. We'll have instructions ready when you call us." He held out his hand to Cyrus and then leaned over Mrs. Pollifax and gave her a quick hug. "Thanks again, and take care of yourselves," he said.

"I'll see you to the door," Cyrus told him, and ushered him out, leaving Mrs. Pollifax alone at the table to stare at the remnants of her egg.

She reflected that the stripes on her back had turned into scar tissue, the nightmares had ceased, and she had been certain that the experience in Hong Kong had in no way affected her spirit.

It hadn't, had it?

A very small errand, she reminded herself. When a person has fallen off a horse . . .

Exactly, she told herself firmly, drew a deep breath and stood up to begin clearing the breakfast dishes from the table. Nevertheless she felt shaken by her sudden attack of anxiety. On his return to the kitchen Cyrus would insist on probing her feelings about Bishop's small errand and she was determined that he not suspect her sudden uneasiness. As she carried dishes across the room and inserted them into the dishwasher she searched for a change in subject to distract him.

When he strolled back into the kitchen she was ready for him and met him with a bright smile. "Cyrus, I had no idea you grew up with a future diplomat, even if he did get murdered. Tell me about him!"

She watched the grave look on his face vanish; Cyrus was chuckling. "Well, he wasn't John Lloyd Matthews in those days," he said. "We called him Joker Matthews. Wasn't very diplomatic then, either, the two of us nearly came to blows any number of times over whether Charley Wexler or Bud Hastings should have won the high school boxing championship. Stubborn as a mule, Joker was."

"But you liked him?" she said, smiling. Hearing about Cyrus' many acquaintances never bored her. She felt, however, that Joker Matthews could not possibly measure up to Slip-Fingered Frank or Deadly Eddy, both of whom Cyrus had represented in court a number of times before he became a judge.

"Liked him very much," he said, and proceeded to tell her all about John Lloyd Matthews, a.k.a. Joker, until she discovered that in distracting Cyrus she had also distracted herself from her doubts; she was ready again for Thailand.

Climbing into his car Bishop placed the attaché case on the seat beside him, started the car and drove down the driveway to enter Route Two. He did not immediately pick up the car phone to report to Carstairs but waited until he had reached a rest area. Pulling into it he called the office and when Carstairs came on the line he said, "It's okay, they've agreed to do it."

"Splendid! No problems?"

"Cyrus balked a little, worried about Emily taking this on so soon after Hong Kong but Mrs. Pollifax, bless her, talked of climbing back on a horse immediately after falling off . . . Now what happened after you sent me dashing off in the middle of our midnight conference, anything new?"

There was a moment of silence and then Carstairs said evenly, "What happened after you left is that Upstairs decided we have to learn who and what Ruamsak is, and—"

"*What?*" shouted Bishop.

"—and therefore, after Emily and Cyrus have made contact with him, he'll be placed under surveillance."

"I don't believe it," gasped Bishop. "That's just what you *don't* want!"

"Placed under surveillance," went on Carstairs without expression, "by a chap recommended Upstairs, the surveillant to be a young man from the Bangkok office by name of McAndrews."

"But he's their computer expert," Bishop said in astonishment.

"I have been told that he's also trained in surveillance."

"Do you believe it? Who on earth Upstairs came up with this brilliant idea? Who did this recommending?"

"Mornajay."

"Mornajay!" exploded Bishop. "By what right?"

Carstairs said coolly, "Since Lance Mornajay is one of my superiors I suppose he has every right, and since he spent ten years in Thailand during the Vietnam War I can only hope he knows what the hell he's doing."

Aha, gloated Bishop, *Carstairs is furious under that brittle calm.*

"McAndrews is to follow Emily and Cyrus from the moment they land at the Chiang Mai airport," he continued, "and thence to the hut off Thapae Road on Thursday."

"I never heard of anything so stupid," protested Bishop. "Does Mornajay understand the risks? Does anyone Upstairs? Don't they realize that if Ruamsak discovers he's being followed we'll never hear from him again, and we lose a damn promising informer?"

"There's no time for sulking, Bishop," Carstairs told him. "If you'll tell me just when Emily and Cyrus arrive in Chiang Mai I'll cable time of arrival to this—this McAndrews."

Bishop caught the distaste in Carstairs' voice and was glad for it. Digging into his attaché case he brought out his notes and repeated the plane's schedule; his lack of sleep was beginning to affect him, and between this and news of Mornajay's interference he felt distinctly irritable.

"All right," Carstairs said, and repeated the hour. "Still parked by the side of the road, Bishop?"

"Of course. Drinking in every pristine word," he said crossly, "and not liking any of it."

"Then I suggest you get moving immediately because all hell's breaking loose again in the Sudan and you're needed. You can sleep on the plane."

"Sleep?" repeated Bishop, starting the car again. "A word vaguely familiar to me, yes, but perhaps as I drive along you could describe it to me, with added descriptions on how it knits the ravel'd sleeve of care and all that?"

But Carstairs had severed the connection. Bishop grinned and settled for the car radio instead and a very loud Jimmie Cliff rendition of "You Can Get It If You Want."

Following that he swore passionately at Mornajay, whom he did not like. Probably nobody did, he thought, but still it was unlike anyone Upstairs to interfere and he shared all of Carstairs' resentment.

Chapter 2

Two days later by the calendar, but only Tuesday in her new time zone, Mrs. Pollifax sat over coffee on the terrace of the Oriental Hotel and gazed with delight at her new surroundings, drawing nourishment from the sight of bougainvillea, jasmine and palm trees, and savoring the warmth of a January day at this opposite corner of the globe. They had arrived late the evening before, and it was noon in Bangkok now, although heaven only knew what time it was at home, probably the middle of the night, she reflected, since she had left Cyrus soundly asleep in their hotel room. She did not feel sleepy at all, or alone either, for the tables slightly below her were filling with people of assorted nationalities; she had already caught snatches of conversation in French, there was a large party of Japanese in one corner and the couple seated behind her were speaking in the clipped accents of the British.

Like a toy paper flower dropped into a glass of water, Mrs. Pollifax felt herself expanding and flowering.

Beyond the terrace the life on the river was equally as interesting to her. Long green ribbons of hyacinth flowed with the current past the terrace and at the moment three barges were passing, each of them with a tiny house perched on its stern. As the barges moved out of view a fantailed sightseeing boat with awnings *put-putted* into midstream, merrily tooting its horn, and before that had disappeared another barge slid into view towing a long line of teak logs on which several men squatted, their colored shirts vivid against the dark wood.

So this is Thailand, she thought dreamily, and then amended this, remembering that most of the country was rural: this was therefore *Bangkok,* which they would presently go out and explore once Cyrus was awake. In the meantime she had already walked out to see the spirit-house that stood at the corner of the hotel to placate any disgruntled spirits, and she had purchased a huge square of Thai silk at a shop across the street. She wore it tied around her head now, although presently it would have to be exchanged for the handwoven straw hat with a wide brim that she had brought with her, because it was growing steadily warmer and more humid. Even as she thought this a pair of waiters began unfurling striped umbrellas to shade each table from the sun.

At the same moment, as if given his cue—and at such a time Mrs. Pollifax felt the world truly was a stage—a young man in baggy trousers and white shirt walked out of the door holding up a large blackboard and ringing a bell as he moved among the tables. On the blackboard in white chalk was printed the name Mrs. Reed-Pollifax: she was being paged. Waving a hand she collected her message, paid her bill and left.

Cyrus was waiting for her in the lobby, looking huge among the less bulky Thai and Japanese around him; he was holding an envelope and looking triumphant. "Plane tickets for Chiang Mai, Emily. Just delivered."

"And you're awake!"

"Awake and ready to see Bangkok."

"Not hungry?"

He smiled drowsily at her. "Cheated . . . called room service and had a luxurious breakfast in the bathtub. Very therapeutic."

"Exactly how holidays should be," she told him, beaming.

"Golden Buddha first?" he suggested as they strolled toward the exit past palm trees set into huge porcelain tubs.

The glass doors were swung open magically for them by a boy in oriental costume. "Cyrus," she breathed, "I do believe he does nothing but open doors all day. Cyrus, could we take a *tuk-tuk* as they call them, one of those motor scooters with a carriage built into it?"

"Later." Cyrus took her arm and said firmly, "I think after seeing all the traffic last night—and they drive like bats out of hell here—we take a taxi. Don't mean to deprive you, m'dear, but I've a horror of being squashed between two buses. The Wat Trimitr—Golden Buddha," he told the cab driver, and they set off to see their first temple.

There was nothing so enlivening, thought Mrs. Pollifax, than to be plunged into a new culture and to grope for a key to its workings. She was to feel later that their visit to the Wat Trimitr summed up many of the contradictions of Bangkok and of Thailand because much to her astonishment the Golden Buddha—made of five and a half tons of pure gold—stood in a temple on the edge of Chinatown near the railway station, on a shabby and congested street that in New York might even be called a slum. Yet there sat the Buddha, huge and massive, its five and a half tons of gleaming gold smiling tranquilly down at those who casually wandered in to bow three times, kneel, leave offerings of paper flowers, ribbons, incense, or to take photographs.

"And not a guard in sight," she whispered to Cyrus.

"But accessible," pointed out Cyrus. "Available to everyone."

She admitted that she liked that, as well as the story behind it: that when it was found it had been a huge *stucco* Buddha, accepted as such until in being moved by a crane it was accidentally dropped, chipping off a corner of the stucco to reveal the glitter of gold underneath. And now it was here, just off a crowded courtyard in a busy temple, and of such value that it boggled the mind.

"But I'd still worry about it," she said, adding earnestly, "I don't mean anyone in Thailand would consider making off with it because it's a sacred relic, but when you think of how art treasures are being stolen everywhere—"

"A bit unwieldy," pointed out Cyrus. "Need a derrick. Then what?"

"I don't know," she said, troubled, "but I'd worry. I don't think they *realize*—"

He smiled at her. "Already thinking how?"

"Of course not," she told him, but she had the grace to blush. "Well," she admitted, "there's perhaps a small amount of the criminal in all of us."

Cyrus' eyes were twinkling. "Speak for yourself, m'dear, but softly, or we'll be hauled off for questioning."

And there it was, she thought ruefully, her imagination was so *lamentably* undisciplined. There had always been an unconventional Emily under the various Mrs. Pollifaxes who had raised two children, grown geraniums, chaired Garden Clubs and poured tea but this odd bent had never been acknowledged, and when it occasionally surfaced it had been considered an aberration, at least until she had begun to work for Carstairs and the Department, where she had discovered that odd bents fitted being a spy very well.

Perhaps, she thought doubtfully, such a perverse way of looking at things was a prerequisite for any agent but she wondered if sometimes it was a little hard on Cyrus. He was very tolerant but, after all, he had been a judge for years, passing sentence on the criminals of the world, and then—absurdly—he had married a woman who held a brown belt in karate and occasionally entered a netherworld where the same laws that Cyrus represented had to be twisted, if not broken. It must strike him as ironic, she thought, but then Cyrus enjoyed irony. Nevertheless she wondered for a brief moment whether her risky assignments for Carstairs might have brought a mutation in her thinking.

After pondering this she decided that she still had scruples and, virtuously, that being aware of how the criminal mind worked was just as important as making blancmange and growing geraniums in her more conventional life. With this decided, for Mrs. Pollifax was conscientious by nature, she dismissed her philosophical doubts and was happy to move on with Cyrus to the Grand Palace.

Here they wandered through an enchanted fairyland of color and glitter, a virtual forest of *chedis* with their pointed spires of gilt, mosaic or gold. Pausing under the sweeping curves of slant-roofed temples they gazed down vista after vista of gilt, blue tile, brilliant frescos, trees, flowers, often interrupted by the tall thin stems of gilt parasols that looked like huge and glorious gold goblets. They came at last to the Temple of the Emerald Buddha where Mrs. Pollifax found herself disappointed because she had expected the Emerald Buddha to be at least the size of the five-and-a-half-ton Golden Buddha but instead it was quite small, it could be measured in inches and was almost obscured by the smoke from joss sticks.

At last, fleeing the rising heat they returned to the hotel where they gave themselves up to other joys of being on holiday, dining in one of the hotel's restaurants and sampling strange exotic foods.

"But spicy," Cyrus commented. "Glad now I brought my sardines."

"Oh, Cyrus, surely not yet?"

"Not yet, no," he said amiably, "but I certainly plan to slip one or two tins into my camera case tonight for easy access. I am," he added unnecessarily, "a large man. I need protein."

She laughed. Later, returned to their room, she laughed again as he tenderly brought out two of his six sardine tins and slid them into his camera bag. She was still smiling as she resumed addressing postcards to her son, Roger, daughter, Jane and to her old neighbor Miss Hartshorne but her thoughts were not entirely on the cheerful messages that she wrote. She was remembering that tomorrow they would fly off to Chiang Mai to meet a man named Ruamsak, and she found herself wondering what Ruamsak was doing and thinking at this hour, and whether he might already be in Chiang Mai waiting for Thursday morning . . .

Chapter 3

Ruamsak came early to the hut behind Thapae Road but he arrived by a circuitous route: he approached it from another alley, making his way to the rear of the house by climbing walls, which alarmed a large family of ducks, and tiptoeing down rows of growing vegetables. He had chosen not to sleep in the hut, which would have saved him money, but had instead spent the night in a hostel run by a Chinese. Yesterday he had checked the house and found it empty but even so he was wary: the hut was built six feet off the ground, of split bamboo and thatch, and he first crept underneath the floor and squatted there, listening for signs that someone might have preceded him. After some minutes, hearing only the harsh click of a gecko, he climbed into the hut by way of the shutterless window in the back, and at once inspected the handfuls of sand that he'd scattered yesterday at the door and under each of the four windows. No one had been here: he looked behind the bamboo screen that ran halfway down the center of the room and then he walked in behind the screen and sat down, cross-legged, to wait.

He was expecting two people in the hours ahead: the unknown person to whom he would deliver his information but first of all the man to whom he had entrusted the letter that was undeniable proof of what he already knew and carried in his head. He had thought for a long time about how to conceal this letter, and he felt that he had been very ingenious in seizing on the use of magic talismans and white magic. He had planned it carefully: first he had trimmed the letter to the size of a *yantra* that he'd borrowed from his sister, one of several that hung by string over her new baby to guard it against evil spirits. Since the *yantra* had been consecrated by the monks he felt that it would guard him, too, against evil spirits, as well as bring him good fortune, and a man could not have too much good fortune. This particular *yantra* was called a *Yan Trinishinghe,* and was a square of paper with four squares drawn diagonally across the main one, leaving half-squares at each corner, with certain mystical numbers and figures inscribed in each space. Behind this he had lightly attached the cutdown letter and had then taken both to an out-of-the-way lacquer factory yesterday. Showing the man the *yantra,* but not the letter concealed behind it, he had rolled the two thin sheets of paper into a tube and asked to have this set into a *phyot* arm-ring.

The man had exclaimed, "This is protection indeed, a *yantra* and a *phyot* arm-ring!"

But despite the money that had been placed on the counter in front of the man he had insisted it could not be done by nightfall. It was true, he said, that weaving a circle of cotton yarn around the tube of paper could be done in an hour or two but the lac that would hold it all together in the shape of an arm-ring needed time in the drying cellar. Failing this, he said, the lac would melt —*laly!*—and there would be nothing the next day but a piece of paper and a handful of cotton yarn. He had been very firm: he was a craftsman, he said, and in such matters was to be trusted.

And so Ruamsak had taken back half the money on the counter, promising it to the man on delivery, promising even more money the earlier in the morning the arm-ring was brought to him, and he had drawn a sketch of the place where he was to bring it.

Except for this delay he felt that he'd done well. Even if the man in the lacquer shop unfolded the rolled-up *yantra* and discovered the letter behind it the words were in a language he wouldn't understand—Ruamsak had made certain of this before choosing the shop—and the man was being well paid. He would arrive before eight—Ruamsak glanced at the slant of the sun outside the window and nodded—and following this he would have the arm-ring to hand over to the stranger who came for it; in return he would be given his gold.

He turned his head; his senses had picked up the faint whisper of cloth and the creak of bamboo: someone was entering the house. Silently he rose to his feet and waited. The footsteps halted and then moved toward the partition, a head appeared and then a man stepped inside the half of the room that Ruamsak occupied.

It was not the man from the lacquer shop; this was someone he'd never seen before and Ruamsak wondered if this was the man to whom he should deliver the letter. He was about to greet him when the man took a step forward and Ruamsak saw the knife in his hand—a killing knife . . .

A chill raced down Ruamsak's spine.

Jacoby, he thought . . . Jacoby must have known all the time, must have been alert enough to know his files had been ransacked, and now he had sent a man to kill him.

He swore at himself for having come unarmed; he had walked into a trap like a bird coaxed into a cage by a handful of rice.

Jai yen yen, he told himself to slow the racing of his heart: *keep your cool.* He waited, knowing there would be others outside as well, and that they would not allow him to leave here alive . . . Death had entered this room.

At ten minutes past eight, with cameras conspicuously in hand, Mrs. Pollifax and Cyrus climbed into a taxi and set out for Thapae Road. They had so far enjoyed Chiang Mai very much, and following their errand on Thapae Road they planned to enjoy the remaining hours even more. Certainly it was a more relaxed city than Bangkok, so relaxed that Cyrus had agreed to ride in a *tuk-tuk* yesterday after their arrival, observing that

Chiang Mai drivers might drive with a certain lightheartedness but with an absence of the frenzy that had dismayed him in Bangkok. In the evening they had dined at the Old Chiang Mai Cultural Center and had then watched tribal dancers perform, and it was here that they'd had a very pleasant talk with a young American named McAndrews, who seemed to be following the same itinerary: his *tuk-tuk* had passed them on the street, he'd been seen in the lobby of their hotel, and in its restaurant, and he had dined at the Cultural Center, too, at which point they had introduced themselves.

A very nice young man, currently working in Bangkok with an American aid program, he said, but it was strange, thought Mrs. Pollifax, how deeply embarrassed he'd seemed when Cyrus first spoke to him.

The morning air was deliciously cool and the distant mountains still a hazy blue. They drove past tree-shaded villas and sleek government buildings until gradually the streets grew narrower and busier and they came to Thapae Road. Mrs. Pollifax, consulting Bishop's memo, kept an eye out for the Apichat Lacquerware Factory until *"There!"* she cried and the taxi drew over to the curb. Paying the driver they stepped out into Thapae Road.

"Thursday morning, and here we are," Cyrus said, and lifted his camera out of its case, nearly spilling out his two sardine cans as well.

"And there's the alley," Mrs. Pollifax pointed out in a low voice.

They had disembarked in front of the lacquer shop, which was open to the street with all sorts of treasures piled on shelves to catch the eye, and the outline of still more in the shadowy rear: lacquer cups, vases, bowls, dishes, trays, chests, jewelry boxes . . . A gnarled little old woman watched them from a chair inside, hands folded tranquilly in her lap. Mrs. Pollifax smiled at her, lifted her camera and snapped a picture, and then turned to photograph the street. *Protective covering,* she thought, as she edged slowly toward the alley.

Cyrus, she saw, was already standing at the edge of the alley-way, his attention captured by a huge earthenware jug placed at the corner of the lacquer shop. "Emily," he called to her, "just look at this! Magnificent, isn't it?"

She joined him and was at once seized by a rare spasm of acquisitiveness. "Wouldn't that look wonderful in our garden at home?" she said eagerly. It was at least four feet high and made of terra-cotta, with a beautifully graceful line to it.

"Water jug, I suppose," Cyrus said. "Cistern?"

"And made entirely by hand, which makes it so lovely. Do you suppose they'd sell it?"

Cyrus looked at her, amused. "And just how do you think you'd carry this back to the United States?"

"Spoilsport," she told him, running an admiring finger over its texture. "Beautiful," she told the old lady seated nearby. "So big!"

The woman beamed and nodded. *"Ka yai!"*

Reluctantly Mrs. Pollifax tore herself away, remembering that she was not here on Thapae Road to admire water jugs. Moving to the entrance of the alley she glanced over her shoulder. "Coming, Cyrus?"

"In just a minute," he said, nodding, and brought up his camera for a snapshot of the terra-cotta jug.

Mrs. Pollifax turned into the alley, nearly colliding with a man running out of it, a shabby-looking Thai in a great hurry who slowed only to avoid running into her. The man brushed against Cyrus, backed away with mumbled apologies, hesitated and then ran away, leaving Mrs. Pollifax to continue unimpeded. Halfway down the alley she stopped and glanced back, surprised to find that Cyrus was not immediately behind her. She saw that he remained at the entrance to the alley, still, with what seemed to her an extremely odd expression on his face. She was tempted to go back and see what mesmerized him but since she was halfway down the alley—and the purpose of their being here was to walk down this alley—she decided not to tempt fate. Not at all the thing, she decided, to stroll down the alley, return to the street and then walk down it again—*much* too conspicuous. She therefore continued on her way, camera in hand, and almost at once caught a flash of brilliant pink ahead. She had reached their destination.

Bougainvillea spilled over the weatherbeaten fence just as described, a brilliant eruption of color in a somber burnt-sienna scene. She walked through the gap in the fence and crossed a small yard of dull red barren earth to confront what looked more like a hut than a house: it leaned slightly to the left, stood high off the ground on posts and was built of bamboo walls with a thatch roof. A doorway had been cut squarely in the center, but lacked a door, she noted, and a square window was placed symmetrically on either side of it. Mrs. Pollifax mounted five steps and peered into a dark, smoke-stained room.

Inserted into the rear wall directly across from her was a square window through which she could see brilliant sunshine, but since not a ray of it entered the room it appeared more like a bright square of tapestry hung on the wall. She stepped inside, and as her eyes began adjusting to the darkness she discovered a room empty of all but broken shards lying here and there. A woven bamboo partition ran halfway down the center. She called softly, "Anybody here?"

There was only silence until a lizard slithered across the floor, startling her.

Where, she wondered, was Cyrus and why was he taking so long to catch up with her?

She walked around the bamboo screen and into a space equally as dim, with another window through which she could see brilliant but unilluminating sunshine. This room was occupied and she stopped when she saw its occupant, whose sleep she was obviously interrupting. He lay on his back in the center of the space, a square of bright cloth flung over his face to keep out the light, although she wondered crossly what light could possibly disturb him in such a dark room. He looked so relaxed—as if sleep had so suddenly overwhelmed him that he'd simply flung himself on the floor—that she hesitated at waking him.

Tactfully she cleared her throat; when this produced no reaction she added, "Good morning!" and then, hoping she pronounced it correctly, *"Sawadee?"*

And then as her eyes drew in more detail they returned to the shape that rose vertically out of his shirt, just over the heart, which at first glance she had assumed to be some intricate Thai design in the shirt. It was not a design: it was a knife.

Mrs. Pollifax stiffened in shock, and then, *"Oh!"* she gasped and rushed forward to kneel beside him.

Gently, fearfully, she removed the square of bright cloth, staring now at the man in horror because his eyes were wide open and unseeing. She put out a hand to feel for a heartbeat, recoiled at the knife imprisoned in his flesh and reached instead for his outflung hand. There was no pulse: Ruamsak was dead.

Outside the room a rooster crowed and some distance away a child called out. She thought, *Carstairs isn't going to like this . . . I don't like it either,* and then, *I must stay calm, there's nothing more to be done.* But as the initial shock passed she realized that of course there was something more to be done: she was going to have to search Ruamsak's body for whatever he had come to give them.

She sat back and stared down at him: a sturdily built man in his thirties, she guessed, a lean hungry face with the high cheekbones of his race, a long jaw, the mouth twisted into a grimace of shock or pain. His clothes were nondescript: dusty black cotton trousers and sandals on his feet, the gray shirt clean except for a seepage of blood around the knife. She wondered how long he'd been dead and reached out for his hand again and found it warm, with no signs of rigor mortis. This was vaguely alarming because it meant that he'd not been dead for long, he might even have been alive when she and Cyrus left the hotel, which meant . . . but she did not want to think of what that meant, the sooner she was out of here the better, *except where was Cyrus?* She slipped her hand into Ruamsak's left trouser pocket and found it empty. Checking the other pocket she drew out four crumpled 25-*baht* notes; none of them looked as if they held a message but she dropped them into her purse to examine later.

It was at this moment, still kneeling beside Ruamsak, that Mrs. Pollifax realized that she and the dead man were not alone in this room, that someone else—someone living—was with them, and was standing in the shadows by the window. The shock of finding Ruamsak dead had sharpened her senses so that she could not mistake the whisper of cloth as someone shifted from one foot to the other. She glanced up, very alert now, and in the corner saw a shape that did not quite blend in with the shadows: it was a shade lighter and its shape was that of a man.

Staring into the corner she slowly rose to her feet. "I know you're there," she said. "Did you kill him?"

A second later she rued her lack of tact because the man who walked out of the shadows looked even tougher than the dead man at her feet, and certainly no one to trifle with. He was as solidly built as a wrestler, with a long puckered scar across one cheekbone. The scar made him look like a brigand, more Chinese than Thai. His trousers were rolled up to his knees, exposing thick muscular calves; his blue shirt was wrinkled, and on his head he wore an incongruous dirty linen hat, narrow-brimmed, and very British, a hat straight out of *My Fair Lady*. The hat was jammed as squarely on his head as the lid on a teapot, which would have struck her as comical if he'd not looked so menacing.

And she was alone with him, separated from him only by the body on the floor. She wished fervently that she could retract the words she'd just spoken, they hung in the air between them, an accusation hurled at a man who was undoubtedly Ruamsak's murderer, and where was *Cyrus?*

The man walked to the body and looked down at it, and then he leaned over and pulled out the knife, which made her shudder. She wondered what karate strikes could possibly have any impact on this man if he planned to kill her next, and she realized that she was too frozen to manage even a scream.

But he remained standing where he was. He examined the

knife and then he pulled out his shirt and wiped the blood from it carefully.

She managed a weak, "Do you know him?"

He lifted his eyes and studied her. "Do you?"

At least he spoke English; she shook her head.

"So why are you here?" he asked, eyes narrowed.

"My husband and I"—what did one say to a murderer?—"we were taking snapshots—" She held up her camera. "And the alley looked interesting, and—"

"Husband," he said harshly. "Where is this husband?"

His eyes were shrewd as they rested on her; he might wear a funny hat and look like a brigand but he was intelligent and she noticed that he'd not replied to either of her questions. "Outside —somewhere," she stammered.

He glanced again at the dead man on the floor between them. "I think we return you to your husband. At once."

This was good news, she wanted very much to be returned to Cyrus but she managed to say bravely, "And will you call the police?"

She thought he looked amused. He shoved the murder knife in his pocket and jerked his head toward the door. "Show me this husband."

She sighed, failing to see why producing Cyrus was so important to him, unless of course he planned to kill her if she was lying. Obviously there were dimensions to this situation that were obscure at the moment but the important thing was to get out of this house and away from this murderous-looking man. She picked up her purse, slung it over her shoulder and walked to the door.

The brilliance outside was like a blow after the darkness of the hut and she paused on the steps to blink. "Cyrus?" she called.

In front of her stood the fence, framed by its mass of bougain-villea, and beyond that lay the alley, and the alley was empty. She hurried toward it, entering with her brigand companion on her heels, and walked quickly toward the street. The first touch of unease was arriving because Cyrus had been going to follow her, he had *not* followed her and where was he?

She reached the huge earthenware jug and stopped. "This is where I last saw him," she said over her shoulder to the man behind her. "He was—just standing here, looking at this." Her eyes moved among the passersby; she turned and looked up and down the road.

"What did he look like?"

"Tall," she said. "Very big, with—" Her glance moved across the street to a dingy blue van which two men were loading, and as her eyes fell on what they were loading she screamed, *"Cyrus!"*

Without a glance at traffic she plunged into Thapae Road to the cacophony of blowing horns and squealing brakes. "Stop!" she cried. "Stop!"

There were startled glances from the men loading the van; they had been clumsily lifting an inert Cyrus so that he could be crammed into the back of the van but he was large and they were small. At the sound of her screams they shoved him brutally inside, slammed shut the doors, raced to the front, jumped into the van and before she could reach it the van was in motion, nearly running her down.

She stopped in the street and stared after the van, trembling with rage and frustration. "Oh how dare they!" she cried. "What is happening here?"

Her companion caught up with her and grasped her by the arm. "Get out of the street!" he said. "That was your husband?"

She nodded with tears in her eyes.

"Then quick—come!"

Chapter 4

"Come where?" she cried angrily. "What do you want of me? That was *Cyrus!*"

"Quickly—to follow!" he cried, pulling her along the sidewalk.

"Oh thank God," she gasped, and ran with him up the street.

"Here," he said, tearing open the door of an ancient truck and she raced around to the other side and jumped into the cab beside him. Wrestling with keys he started the engine, turned in a broad arc and careered across oncoming traffic, barely avoiding being run down by a bus, a move made even more unnerving because Mrs. Pollifax had forgotten that in Thailand cars drive on the left side of the road.

"Can you see them?" she shouted into his ear as they took off in pursuit of the blue van.

"Yes, they have turned right," he shouted back, and ignoring a stop sign he swerved recklessly across traffic to turn right.

"I see them!" she cried, crouching on the edge of her seat. "They've turned to the left."

They followed to the left, one wheel of their truck bouncing over a curbstone; they turned right and then left again, motorcycles, scooters and bicycles parting in front of them like the Red Sea, cars screaming to a halt, people racing to the side of the road, her companion huddled over the steering wheel with one hand on the horn, the blue van remaining tantalizingly at a distance. It was a perilous neighborhood in which to give chase because it was the old section of town where people slowly crossed the street, even pausing to gossip until van and truck raced down on them and scattered them. She was aware of street stalls, narrow alleys, open-air markets selling cotton fabrics, baskets, cooking pots, heaps of fish and greens, tiny shops bright with gilt Buddhas, incense, paper flowers, votives, men squatting over sidewalk braziers. Suddenly they were back on a road that broadened into a boulevard, passing a school, a college, a bridge over the river Ping and a marker on the edge of the road that announced route numbers.

"They're getting away, we're losing them!" she cried, leaning forward. "Can't you go faster?"

He murmured something unintelligible.

"What?"

"My truck, it can't go faster—it's old."

He was right, of course, it had made horrible noises from the very beginning, reducing them both to shouting, but she refused defeat. After all, Cyrus was in that blue van, for what reasons she couldn't conceive, and to lose sight of the van was to lose Cyrus. "Go faster anyway," she begged, biting her lip in frustration. *Faster, faster,* she whispered over and over to herself, but as she whispered her incantations the blue van added a burst of speed and sped around a curve out of sight.

"Damn," she cried, and the man beside her turned his head and gave her a startled glance.

The road narrowed now as they headed north, and having left the outskirts of the city the villas and the thatch houses thinned out and the trees moved in closer to the road. Looking ahead she realized there would be still more curves as they began climbing toward the hills, and the truck was making fresh sounds of protest as the grade steepened. If Chiang Mai had been higher in altitude than Bangkok she began to understand that even higher altitudes lay ahead, and that the mountains in the hazy distance were precisely where the blue van was heading. It was not a comforting thought.

It was at this moment that Mrs. Pollifax realized the odds against their catching up with the van in this noisy, rattling old truck. It was also the moment when it first occurred to her that she was rushing off into the unknown with a man about whom she knew nothing except that they'd met over a dead body, which was scarcely a recommendation, and her recklessness suddenly appalled her: how could she have done it? It was true that this man had shown a remarkable presence of mind—rather too remarkable, she thought now, uneasily—but he was a complete stranger to her, and she'd certainly joined forces with him very casually and without so much as a thought. No, not casually, she amended: *desperately.* But still, when she considered the circumstances under which she'd met this—this brigand in the My Fair Lady hat—there was little doubt that she was traveling with a killer, and with him she was being taken farther and farther away from Chiang Mai. At this thought a new wave of panic swept over her to add weight to her panic over Cyrus.

She forced herself to breathe deeply and to concentrate on objects. She thought, *The truck rattles, the dashboard is orange with rust, there are hollows in this seat under me as if a dog has been digging for a bone he buried there* . . . Stealing a glance at her companion's profile she found his face grim but determined, and since she was equally as determined she told herself that whoever he was he seemed as eager as she was to catch up with the blue van and this was what mattered the most just now. After riding in silence for nearly half an hour she cleared her throat and shouted at him, "What do we do if we find the blue van?"

He shrugged. "Do? I have the knife in my pocket."

"It was a strange knife," she shouted back at him. "Made by hand, wasn't it? The handle had string or fishing cord wrapped around the wood."

"Around bamboo," he shouted back. "It was a Shan knife."

A Shan knife. She gave him a startled glance but said nothing —shouting was tiresome and in any case a knife made by Shans seemed no more bizarre to her than her circumstances. Checking her wristwatch she saw that it was already half past nine and she decided that if they did not spot the blue van again soon she would insist on being taken to a police station. With this thought she opened her purse and checked money and passport; the police would want to see her passport but what would they make of her story, she wondered, and how much dared she tell them? There was also the pressing question—she could not avoid it indefinitely—as to whether this man would *allow* her to go to a police station or whether she herself had been made captive. She returned the passport to the zippered inside pocket of her purse and was appalled to feel the shape and weight of the gold-laden votive concealed there. She thought wildly, *Perhaps I can use it now to ransom Cyrus . . . if this man doesn't rob me first.* To distract her thoughts from such unpleasant speculations she shouted, "Where does this road go?"

"Chiang Rai," he shouted back.

Chiang Rai . . . and they had just left Chiang Mai, which made for rather a lot of Chiangs. She brought out and unfurled the map she'd crumpled into her purse that morning and set out to make sense of where they were going. She found the Chiang Mai they'd left behind them, and moving her finger northward she discovered the Chiang Rai toward which they were heading, and at the top, near the border, a town called Chiang Saen. Three such Chiangs were almost more than could be dealt with: Mai, Rai and Saen, she repeated to herself, memorizing them, and put the map away with a sigh.

Deprived of conversation she began to examine the countryside through which they were driving, thinking how thrilling it would be if Cyrus were beside her and they were tourists again. They were now in real country, climbing steadily, with hills rising all around them and jungles of palm and secondary growth on either side. There were no houses: tall grasses lined the road, and beyond them the palms, thick undergrowth and then the jungle. The hills scalloping the horizon looked like cutouts from an ancient Chinese print, as if watercolor had been roughly splashed over their peaks to run raggedly down the sides, leaving an impression of unkempt fur. Up ahead a man suddenly walked out of the tall grass and crossed the road. He wore a blue shirt and pants and a round white shoulder bag that crossed his shoulder to rest against his thigh, a circle of artistic white against the blue. Over his shoulder he carried what looked like a very long thin pointed fishing rod. As they swept past him she turned to look and saw that it was not a fishing rod.

"Was that a rifle?" she shouted at her companion.

"Single-shot—*pern yao,*" he shouted back. "Farmers allowed them for hunting here in North."

Watching the man disappear, her head still turned, she saw a motorcycle behind them at some distance and was relieved to find this not quite so lonely a road after all. Nevertheless, having not caught a glimpse of the blue van for a number of miles she decided it was time to confront her companion and demand a police station.

"It's after ten o'clock," she told him, and when he didn't hear her she repeated in a shout, "It's nearly quarter past ten and we've lost the blue van, I want to talk to you!"

"Talk?" He turned and gave her a measuring glance that she found sinister. "Soon," he shouted back, and pointed to a rushing mountain brook on their right. "Stop soon, up ahead."

A mile down the road he slowed the truck and pulled into a clearing. Several other trucks were parked here beside an open thatch-roofed building; beyond, down near the stream of water, stood more huts. The ignition was turned off, the engine gave a last sputter, a gasp, and Mrs. Pollifax could hear again. "Ten minutes," he said, climbing out of the truck.

"But why are you going, and where? We'll lose the van," she cried. She was seeing him full-face again and he looked no less dangerous and intimidating. Perhaps it was the scar, she thought, as well as his bulk, but she found that she preferred the profile that she'd been seeing for the past hour and ten minutes.

"This is Hot Springs Development," he told her. "We may as well use lavatory and pick up food."

"And talk," she reminded him, giving him a hostile glare.

She waited outside the truck while he strolled over to the thatch hut; when he came back he was carrying a wire basket with half a dozen eggs, a handful of bananas and three bottles of cola. With a jerk of his head he summoned her to follow him down to the mountain stream where a shallow cistern had been placed in the water. To her surprise she saw steam rising in clouds: this really was a hot spring. Lowering the basket of eggs into the cistern her companion nodded to her and walked away, presumably to a lavatory.

Mrs. Pollifax paced up and down beside the stream and the eggs, feeling that a great deal of time was being wasted and then, deciding to be sensible, she went off in search of a lavatory too. When she emerged he was waiting, the eggs apparently cooked; he led her to a shaded table, sat down on a bench and handed her a boiled egg.

Fingering it without appetite she said, "I don't even know your name."

He bowed his head slightly. "Bonchoo."

"Bonchoo what?"

"Well—the rest of it is Chalermtkarana," he said dryly, "but we do not bother with two names here. You also have a name?"

"Oh," she said. "Emily Pollifax." Thirsty, she stretched out a hand for one of the colas and took a sip. "Mr. Bonchoo—"

"Just Bonchoo will do."

"All right . . . Bonchoo, we have lost the blue van with my husband inside it and now I wish to be taken to a police station, please, to report this."

He was peeling an egg with expert fingers. "We passed one ten miles back."

"Ten miles—" She looked at him, exasperated. "You must realize my husband's been kidnapped, why didn't you stop?"

"We were following the blue van."

"Which is now far ahead of us," she pointed out indignantly. "And for that matter," she added, unleashing all of her uneasiness in a burst of anger, "for that matter why is it that *you* want to follow the blue van? *You* didn't lose a husband."

Bringing out the Shan knife he sliced his egg neatly and efficiently in half. "This is difficult situation," he said, "and we are losing time. As a good Buddhist is it not possible I wish to gain merit by helping?"

"Well," she snapped, "you can gain merit by taking me now to a police station. They can send out an alert, and find and stop the van."

He said with a shrug, "Maybe so, yes, but I know the men in the blue van—"

"You *know* them?" she gasped.

"You understand not personally," he said, "but since I know where they come from I know where they will go. As for you—" he shrugged. "You go to the police and by the time you explain everything the van will have passed the police check up ahead and will be in Chiang Rai. Also by the time you have explained where and how your husband was kidnapped," he added casually, "and about the dead man you found, it will be *very* late."

He meant, of course, that she was guilty of not reporting Ruamsak's murder at once. *Pure blackmail,* she thought scornfully. "And how would *you* propose to find my husband?"

He said evenly, "I would look for the peoples who drive the van."

"How would you know where to find them?"

"I told you, I know the country where they go."

"How?" she demanded. "Why?"

"Because I live there, I come from the north."

"Did the dead man live in the north, too?" When he didn't reply she said, "You killed him, didn't you?"

He shrugged. "He's dead, does it matter?"

She said angrily, "It matters very much your knowing the men who kidnapped Cyrus and I think you're deliberately delaying my visit to the police so those men in the van can get away. After all, once I tell the police about the murder you'll be the first person they look for, isn't that true?"

He sighed heavily. "You want to know why not the police?"

"I would *love* to know why not the police," she said bitterly. "If, that is, you can possibly find a reason."

He said calmly, peeling another egg, "Because the man who was killed in the house in Chiang Mai was not a nice man. Because the men who took away your husband are not nice men. The police do not always find such men—not here in the north, anyway. And when they look it takes time, much time, and sometimes much—" He hesitated and then said, "much push," but she did not believe that was the word he'd been going to use.

She said abruptly, "And you—are you also not a nice man?"

He said calmly, "Not a nice man at all."

She thought he was deliberately baiting her. "Why were you in Chiang Mai?" she asked.

He shrugged. "I told you, my name is Bonchoo, I went to Chiang Mai with a friend on business, I leave now for home." He looked at her almost with sympathy; certainly he seemed to find her amusing. "But you had better make your choice because I cannot wait, I have waited long enough, the ten minutes passed five minutes ago."

She gave him a furious glance. She was in over her head and she knew it: she was being asked to trust—or not trust, but accompany—a man who appeared to know a great deal more than she did and who was probably a murderer, which made it impossible to trust him, but if Cyrus had been kidnapped by men who were not—as this Bonchoo put it—*nice* men, then it was possible that a man like Bonchoo really could find Cyrus. What was being suggested was that she ignore conventional avenues of help and continue on with Bonchoo, who was no better than he should be, all on the theory—doubtful, surely—that he knew the men who had abducted Cyrus.

She thought, *Don't be a fool, Emily, go to the police.*

She was remembering Hong Kong now, and the enormous confidence with which she had walked into what had turned out to be a trap, and she was also remembering the consequences.

Bonchoo could very well be working for the men in the blue van, and this too could be a trap.

She said accusingly, "You're asking me to trust you?"

He looked astonished. "Trust? Why should you trust me?"

His reply was so reasonable that she gaped at him—what a frustrating rascal he was!—yet at the same time his words shocked her back into her old self with a glimpse of a world that she recognized, a world that she'd entered before, a world without rules, guarantees or trust in anyone but herself, where choices were a gamble, as choices always were, but in this case heavily scored with risk. It was an underground world. If what Bonchoo said was true, then the van and Cyrus were speeding north while she sat here tiresomely debating the character of this man and looking for guarantees.

There were no guarantees. There never had been and there never could be.

She said crisply, "Then let's go." Picking up her purse, hard-boiled eggs, bananas and cola she added, "But if we can't find the blue van in Chiang Rai then I warn you—I go to the police."

"Who's to stop you?" he said mildly, plucking his last egg from the table and rising.

She gave him one last indignant glance and strode back to the truck. At the long thatch-roofed hut where Bonchoo had purchased food a young man turned his head to watch her. She gave him a brief sidelong glance: a mop of dark hair framing a dark face made darker by his bright red shirt, so young she guessed he was not out of his teens. His companion slouched next to him, his back turned to her, his shirt a bright yellow. Their motorcycle—and this she glanced at admiringly—stood parked beside them.

Joining her in the cab of the truck Bonchoo inserted his key in the ignition and then froze, his eyes fixed on the rearview mirror. He looked suddenly grim. "I thought they passed us—they *did* pass us, they have come back, the *naklengs.*"

"The who?" asked Mrs. Pollifax.

"The two hoodlums on the motorcycle."

She looked at him in surprise. "Those two boys? Why do they bother you?"

He said evenly, "Because they have been following behind us since Thapae Road in Chiang Mai . . . They take much care to not pass us, which is not so easy with such a motorcycle. I am thinking when they do pass us they plan mischief to us . . ."

Chapter 5

In Langley, Virginia, it was evening and Carstairs had stayed late to wrap up the day's work. Bishop had departed for dinner, and for the moment the office was quiet as a different half of the world settled down for the night, although not necessarily to sleep: sudden assassinations would continue and information still be passed discreetly in bistros, pubs and bars but only the most vital calls would be put through to him during the night and he thought that only news from Bashir Ilariyo in the Sudan was likely to curtail or interrupt his sleep.

Since in Thailand it was already Thursday morning he was also expecting confirmation from Mrs. Pollifax that Ruamsak's package was safely in hand, and thinking about this he took a last sip of coffee and leaned back in his chair, fervently hoping that Ruamsak would prove too clever for McAndrews, who had been assigned the job of surveillance. It seemed to him a crude mistake to attempt identification of Ruamsak, and he failed to understand Mornajay's obsession about this. Ruamsak had already proved valuable and it was difficult getting information these days about the situation in the north of Thailand. The CIA office in Bangkok had slipped badly, devoting its time mainly to feeding data into computers, as witness McAndrews the computer expert. The

Drug Enforcement Agency—DEA—worked in the north and shared pertinent information but their reports usually concerned the politics of drug smuggling, and who was who among the warlords and drug merchants. He thought of the years that Jacoby had sent them information from Chiang Saen; the department knew, of course, that he had a drug problem but according to Ruamsak the man was entering the terminal stages of opium addiction and, what was worse, to support his habit he was selling information to the Vietnamese in Laos as well as to the CIA. Ruamsak had also thrown doubt on the accuracy of that information. He had written: *I am seeing copies of what he sends to you, they are not right, sir, he changes truth. This I know for I am one who brings to him the news he sells you.* Ruamsak had gone on to correct the misinformation that Jacoby had sent and this had been enlightening, to say the least.

In the adjacent room a door opened and closed and he glanced up to see Bishop beaming at him, his sheepskin jacket dusted with snow. "Thought you might still be here," he said cheerfully. "Stopped in to see—"

He waited because a red light had surfaced on the phone box, followed by a quiet buzz, and Carstairs picked up the receiver. Into the phone he said, "Carstairs here." To Bishop he said, "To see what?"

"See what you've heard from our friend Mrs. P . . . she's checked in okay?"

Carstairs gestured to him to sit down. "Perfect timing, Betsy reports a call from Chiang Mai coming through right now."

"Wonderful," said Bishop, and sat down and picked up the extension, smiling in anticipation. His smile faded as he heard the voice that came on the line; it was not Mrs. Pollifax, it was a man's voice, piercing and distraught, and it was saying, "I was given this number to call if—my name's McAndrews, sir, and—"

Bishop experienced a sinking sensation in his stomach. He thought, *Something's gone wrong.*

Carstairs reached over to switch on a machine and record this. Interrupting the rush of words he said sharply, "Pull yourself together, McAndrews, I can't understand what you're saying, you seem to be babbling about a body?"

"Yes, yes, body," repeated McAndrews frantically. "Sir, I've never been in such a situation before, and I can't reach—"

Body, thought Bishop, suddenly very still.

"Breathe deeply," counseled Carstairs. "Better still, begin at the beginning. You were assigned two people to follow in Chiang Mai, a man and a woman, right?"

At the other end McAndrews could be heard taking deep breaths, and they waited patiently. "Yes, sir," he said at last. "Except it didn't—but to begin at the beginning, sir, I followed them to this place on Thapae Road. That was an hour ago, it's not quite nine in the morning here."

"And?"

"Well, the lady went down this alley while the gentleman—Mr. Reed, is it?—stopped to admire a jug—"

"A what?"

"Water jug, sir. Large water jug outside a lacquer shop. So I waited, thinking he'd join his wife or she'd join him in a few minutes but these two men walk up to Mr. Reed and start talking, very pleasantly, too—"

"American?"

"No, Thai. And although I could see that Mr. Reed wanted to pull away they just kept talking with him, and then suddenly he sagged—only word for it, sir, a big man like that. The two men catch him and sort of pull and drag him across the street to a van, which took a while, what with the size of him, and all the traffic, and just as they're trying to get him into the rear of the van—to take him off to a hospital, I thought—his wife came out of the alley, screamed 'Cyrus!' and the men slammed the doors shut, hopped in and took off."

Carstairs said sharply, "Was Reed conscious or unconscious? What condition was he in?"

"Dopey at first, unconscious by the time they reached the van."

Under his breath Carstairs began swearing. "Go on."

"Yes . . . Well, the lady's in the middle of the street, cars stopping and people shouting, and this chap who followed her out of the alley—"

"What chap? She was with someone?"

"Yes, and he takes her by the arm, pulls her to a truck and they hop in and take off after the van."

Carstairs gritted his teeth. "And you did what? McAndrews, are you calling to tell me—"

"That's it, sir," groaned McAndrews. "My own car was parked too far down the street, very discreetly, you understand, so by the time I got to it both the truck and the van were gone. I drove up and down streets looking for them but there was no sign of them so I came back and parked the car and went down the alley to take a look at where the lady had gone, and there was this hut, and—" His voice broke.

"Yes yes," Carstairs said impatiently.

"That's where I found it."

"Found what?"

"The body, sir. The only occupant of the house was—is—a dead man, Thai or Chinese, on the floor with a knife wound in his ribs and his body still warm."

"Good God," Carstairs said, his mind racing ahead to form pictures of Mrs. Pollifax either committing a murder or witnessing a murder.

In a rage, Bishop flung himself out of his chair and began pacing back and forth. *The fool,* he thought furiously, *any fool would have realized that Reed was being kidnapped, not taken to a hospital, and any fool would have made a dash for his car—if he'd been so stupid as to not have it nearby and ready . . . Christ!*

"What you do next," Carstairs said evenly, "is find them, McAndrews. Check the hospitals and see if anyone answering Reed's description has been brought in, which I doubt very much, but it's the first thing to establish. Then go back to Thapae Road and question people, see if anyone can identify the two men who carried off Reed, or if anyone recognized the man with Reed's wife. There must have been dozens of witnesses, see if you

can find out what happened to Reed, what made him collapse
. . . I suspect a hypodermic needle . . . Don't call in the police
yet, get facts."

"Yes, sir. I'm terribly sorry, sir."

"Done much surveillance before, McAndrews?" he inquired in
a silky voice.

"No, sir, only in training. This is my first job."

Carstairs looked appalled. "I see . . . well . . ." He sighed.
"Since you're already on the scene and know the cast of characters there's no point in bringing in anyone more experienced just
now. Report back to me, McAndrews, and try to remember we're
pinning all our hopes on you. *Find* them!"

He hung up and met Bishop's blazing eyes. "Pinning all our
hopes on him!" exploded Bishop. "The man's obviously a klutz
and you know—you know damn well what I told Mrs. Pollifax, I
told her—I assured her—they've *both* disappeared now?"

"Gently, Bishop."

"Gently, hell," snarled Bishop. "Are you forgetting Hong
Kong? I told both of them this was a simple courier operation, I
gave them my word—just pick up the package and—what are
you doing?"

Carstairs had picked up the phone. He said, "Just because I'm
not having a tantrum, Bishop, doesn't mean that I'm any less
enraged than you. This was Mornajay's inspiration, and it's
Mornajay's head that I'd like on a platter. Betsy, connect me
with Upstairs . . . Mornajay's office, Southeast Asia division,
and if he's left I want to know precisely where to contact him."

"That's more like it," Bishop said with feeling, and stopped
pacing and sat down. He listened to Carstairs, suave and courte-
ous now as he spoke with Mornajay's assistant and asked where
Mornajay could be reached. There was a pause and then Carstairs said firmly, "But I must reach him, Mrs. Hudson. You
were at the conference last Saturday night—the Ruamsak affair
—so you'll know why I need to talk to him when I tell you that
all hell seems to have broken loose over there, and—what?"

Carstairs looked startled. "Don't know *what?* Yes of course I'll wait . . ." He hung up, looking puzzled. "Put some coffee on, Bishop, she's coming down here."

Bishop was equally as startled. "For pete's sake why?"

Carstairs was frowning. "I don't know, but she says she can't tell me where to reach Mornajay and she sounds upset."

Bishop went out to his office and reheated stale coffee and when Mrs. Hudson arrived he ushered her in to Carstairs and handed her a cup of the brew.

"Thank you," she said, placing it on the desk but making no move to touch it.

She was a plump and capable woman with sandy hair worn in a bun, a no-nonsense person famous for her efficiency; now Bishop was astonished to see tears in her eyes.

"I simply haven't known what to do," she was saying in an anguished voice, "and I simply have to tell someone, Mr. Carstairs. Mr. Mornajay has absolutely disappeared and I haven't seen him since Monday. He left the office in the middle of a ten o'clock appointment—just walked out and never came back. I've been doing everything possible to cover for him—lying, working nights to keep up, stalling people . . . I've checked all the hospitals, Mr. Carstairs, I've even contacted Minneapolis, where he still has an aunt living."

And this is Wednesday evening, realized Bishop, jarred by her disclosure.

Carstairs was frowning. "This certainly doesn't sound like Mornajay, he's not done this before, has he?"

"Never," she said passionately. "Always at his desk, except for his vacations, and I've worked with him for thirteen years now. I feel I can trust you with this, and frankly I need help, he's got to be found!"

Carstairs looked puzzled, his fingers tapping the desk as he considered what could only be a bombshell in Bishop's estimation. He said quietly, "Tell me about Monday morning, Mrs. Hudson."

"Yes, of course," she said.

"You say he left in the middle of an appointment?"

She nodded. "I've gone over and over it, Mr. Carstairs. There was a phone call that he accepted, in spite of that appointment, and soon after that he simply walked out without explanation. It was a phone call from Bangkok."

Carstairs' eyebrows shot up. "Bangkok! Any idea who from?"

"Yes, from a woman named Chin-Ling."

"Someone he's in regular contact with?"

She shook her head. "You mean an operative—no, the name's not one of ours, I've looked into that. I remember her name very clearly because I told her he was busy, tied up with an appointment. She said it was terribly important and begged me to tell him that Chin-Ling was calling, so I did, and—I must confess I was surprised—he said he'd talk to her at once."

"And it was after this that he left? How long did he and Chin-Ling talk?"

"I suppose that would be important, yes. Let's see . . ." She closed her eyes, thinking back. "I'd guess about five minutes but there'd be a record of it down at switchboard."

At this moment Bishop would have given a week's wages to know what Carstairs was thinking and how much of his reaction he would share. Carstairs was a man who operated on intuition as well as logic; it was what made him special. For himself, he was baffled as to what could possibly lead to Mornajay's mysterious disappearance; he was certainly not a man given to whimsical impulses or to any spontaneity at all; he was a man who seemed to have no private life and to live totally for his work.

Bishop listened to Carstairs quietly tell Mrs. Hudson that he would use his contacts discreetly to locate Mornajay, that she was not to worry, that he was glad she had told him of Mornajay's disappearance and that he would not betray her confidence. When she had left, Carstairs gave Bishop a long and thoughtful glance. He said, grimly, "This is completely out of character for Mornajay."

Bishop nodded and reached for the cup of coffee that Mrs. Hudson had left untouched.

There followed a long silence and then abruptly Carstairs

snapped his fingers. Picking up the phone he asked to be put through to Bangkok, to the U.S. Embassy first, and then to the CIA, which occupied an office in the same building. Since the phone in Bishop's office was buzzing he did not hear what happened next; when he returned, Carstairs was sitting at his desk staring at his desk blotter.

"I surprised them very much," Carstairs told him with a strange little smile. "Neither the Embassy nor the CIA have any knowledge of Mornajay being in Bangkok. They wondered why he would be."

Bishop said in astonishment, "You think *that's* where he is?"

"He had that call from Bangkok," mused Carstairs. "If he's not at work in his office, not hit by a car and in the hospital, not in his apartment and not in Minneapolis—" He stopped, adding thoughtfully, "He spent nearly ten years in Thailand during the Vietnam War, you know."

Bishop said bitterly, "Lining up people like McAndrews?"

Carstairs gave him a long and interested look. "Exactly . . . Now while I sign these last papers and file them, Bishop, put me through to Bangkok again, will you? This time to a place on Patpong Road called the Indiana 500." Seeing Bishop's face he added kindly, "A bar where expatriates and foreign newsmen hang out. I want to speak to the owner, Chuck Holloway."

"Right, sir."

The call and the connection came through quickly and Bishop frankly eavesdropped. He heard Carstairs and Holloway greet each other cordially, and following a few inquiries about business at the Indiana 500—booming but not like in the old days—he heard Carstairs ask if Holloway remembered Lance Mornajay.

Holloway laughed. "Who could forget him? Mr. Know-It-All we called him. How could I forget a guy who always had to tell me how to fix a margarita? Sure I remember the guy."

Carstairs asked if by any chance he'd seen Mornajay recently. *Ridiculous,* thought Bishop, and then his jaw dropped as Chuck Holloway said, "Sure, he was in here just last night. I didn't speak to him, he was with another guy, and in heavy conference

over in a corner, you know? Here about—not long, maybe forty
minutes. Late last night it was, *very* late."

Bishop thought that even Carstairs sounded startled at this
news. "We're talking about the same man, you're certain?" he
asked.

"Sure I'm certain. Haven't seen Mornajay for a long time but
the same mop of curly gray hair and cold blue eyes, and damned
if the barmaid didn't say he ordered a margarita. Cold as ice and
an ego a mile wide, that man."

"That's Mornajay," Carstairs said, and "Thanks, Chuck, keep
this under your hat, will you?"

"You bet."

So Mornajay was in Bangkok, thought Bishop, staggered by
this information. As Carstairs hung up Bishop shook his head
and said, "What on God's green earth is Mornajay doing over
there—strictly on the sly—when he has operatives and field men
to do the work?"

Carstairs said slowly, "Totally out of character, which makes it
very interesting, don't you think?"

"Not to me," Bishop said, scowling. "Does he know who you
sent to Chiang Mai to pick up Ruamsak's package?"

Carstairs shook his head. "Only a nameless man and woman
from our courier list."

"So he hasn't gone to rescue Emily and Cyrus."

Carstairs gave a short bark of a laugh. "Scarcely, no. But he's
there, Bishop."

Bishop nodded.

"And he *shouldn't* be there." Carstairs frowned. "I don't like
it, Bishop. I don't like the sound of it and I don't like the smell of
it either." He added grimly, "In the space of a few hours we've
lost Mrs. Pollifax, we've lost Cyrus, and in all probability it was
Ruamsak dead in that hut, and now one of our top men Upstairs
gives every evidence of having gone berserk."

"Trouble," Bishop said flatly, and sighed.

Chapter 6

Mrs. Pollifax, hearing that a motorcycle had kept pace with them since Thapae Road, wondered if she believed Bonchoo. She could see no reason why they should be followed, and in spite of their brief conference she couldn't fathom Bonchoo's motives; there remained any number of scenarios that could explain him and she disliked almost all of them. There might have been an amused glint in his eye back at the hot springs—and humor implied intelligence—but she had met her share of thoroughly wicked people who were intelligent and sometimes even humorous. She thought Bonchoo very adroit at concealing himself, and no matter how she tried to overlook the scar across his face it continued to suggest a life of violence. Worse, he'd made no attempt to reassure her, and had already admitted that he was no better than the men who had stolen Cyrus.

Nevertheless his suspicions about the two men on the motorcycle left her uneasy and after they had driven a mile or two at their slow and stately pace she found herself turning her head to look at the road behind them, and it was proof of her unease that she turned her head very slowly and carefully.

The motorcycle was behind them again. And motorcycles, she reflected, did not customarily drive at thirty-five miles an hour, and hang back from passing. Giving Bonchoo a sharp glance she said, "Friends of yours?" and was immediately sorry that she'd said this because she discovered him looking intensely worried, an expression she'd not seen on his face before, and since she was worried too it gave them something in common. When he didn't reply to her flippant remark she shouted at him, "How far now to Chiang Rai?"

"One and one half hours," he shouted back, and returned to his thoughts, which were obviously dark ones.

She was certain by now that some unidentifiable metal object must have been tossed into the engine to produce the groans and rattles that made conversation exhausting. She occupied herself by turning her head every few minutes to check the motorcycle's presence behind them, and behind them it remained, the splash of red shirt reappearing after every curve in the road, and always at the same distance behind them. Her watch told her that it was a quarter to eleven now; for half an hour she continued doing this, aware that beside her Bonchoo's eyes also strayed frequently to his rearview mirror. They reached a small plateau, passing rice paddies and two thatch-roofed houses. A woman carrying baskets on a pole across her shoulders walked toward them across the fields—she was glimpsed and then she was gone—and the road began climbing again through the forest.

They had driven for another fifteen minutes in silence when Bonchoo suddenly shouted to her in an agonized voice, "I am going to stop, they follow behind us like *fahrawng*—thunderclouds! It puts butterflies in my stomach."

"Stop?" she repeated doubtfully. "But why?"

"I must!" He looked really upset.

"But they stay behind us," she shouted back at him. He was slowing the truck, its rattles subsiding; she thought he was choosing a very poor place to honor his butterflies because the road was alarmingly empty and the forests on either side dense. "What if they stop, too?" she asked.

"I have to find out," he cried. "If they are after us like bandits they will stop us anyway, soon or late, and it will be in a place *they* choose."

She nodded; this she could understand. "What do you suggest doing?"

"There is a monkey wrench there," he said, pointing under her seat. "A big one."

She leaned over and brought it out as he steered the truck to the side of the road. When he turned off the engine the silence was so startling that it fairly screamed at her.

"Stay," he said, taking the monkey wrench from her and opening the door beside him. "I am going into the bushes—they'll think for the usual reason. You'll be safe in the truck. Lock the doors and stay."

He slid out of the truck and a second later vanished into the dusty vines and tangles along the road, a few low palms quivering behind him. Mrs. Pollifax thought it gallant of him to insist that she remain in the truck and she thought the better of him for it, but she could not feel that being confined between a door and a gearshift would prove very interesting. If what Bonchoo suspected was true then she certainly didn't relish watching two young men descend upon Bonchoo in the forest, outnumbering him. It seemed pertinent to her own future to lighten the odds and become a presence on the scene.

She stepped out of the truck just as the motorcycle overtook them. It slowed to a stop, which was either Samaritan-like or ominous, except that after a glance at the dark and hostile faces of the two young men she decided that it was ominous. Mrs. Pollifax nodded politely to them and strolled around the truck to kick a tire, observing them discreetly as she pretended concern for the tire. The two men exchanged words in Thai, laughed, climbed off the motorcycle, pushed down the kickstand and strolled to the edge of the road. Peering into the woods they exchanged more words and then Red Shirt parted the shrubbery and went in after Bonchoo, leaving the other man at the edge of the road to watch him disappear and to wait.

So Bonchoo was right, she thought, her heart beginning to beat

faster, her adrenalin glands on the alert. She casually walked over
to join the man at the edge of the road. "Good morning," she
said conversationally. "Perhaps you can tell me how far it is to
Chiang Rai now?"

He turned and gave her an impatient glance. He didn't reply
and she thought his eyes held an unhealthy joy as he stood and
waited. With a shrug he turned back to the forest, and Mrs.
Pollifax retreated several paces behind him and waited, too. Presently there came a cry, a scuffle, a grunt followed by a groan, a
voice shouting, and Red Shirt's companion stiffened and took a
step forward. He had overlooked Mrs. Pollifax, however, who
had already assumed the basic stance that her instructor Lorvale
called *hachiji-dachi*. Lifting her right arm, hand open, she struck
the back of the man's neck with a quick decisive karate slash that
sent him sprawling unconscious to the ground.

There was a thrashing of dried grass and Bonchoo leaped out
of the bushes, knife in one hand, monkey wrench in the other, a
bloody gash across his scarred cheek. He came to a halt, gaping
at the young man lying at her feet. "But—what happened?" he
gasped.

She said calmly, "I hit him."

"You?" He looked from the man on the ground to Mrs. Pollifax and his mouth dropped open. "You—are you a witch?"

"Karate, brown belt," she said crisply. "What about the other
one?"

"Knocked out with the monkey wrench but he was a tough
one. He is still breathing, thank God, or I would have lost much
merit." He sank down on a rock and put his head in his hands
and to her surprise she saw that he was trembling. "I—
Bonchoo," he groaned. "To say Bonchoo is scared—*mai dai,* not
good. This is not an auspicious day for me!"

He suddenly seemed surprisingly human to her. She could
sympathize with him—it was not an auspicious day for either of
them—but she could be sympathetic only to a modest level. She
said accusingly, "If they belong to the men who kidnapped Cyrus

they should have gone after *me* but they didn't, they wanted to kill *you,* Bonchoo. Why?"

He was not listening. He struck his forehead with a fist. "I didn't see, I didn't know—there is one smart man behind this, and me, I am amateur."

"Well, I'm not," she told him sharply.

He glanced up at her and then at the man lying unconscious on the ground; he said dryly, "No—no, you are not amateur and this I do not understand either."

"Who is the 'smart man' behind this?" she demanded.

He shook his head. "He was crafty as a *naga* to send *gawng john* after me."

"I do think we should get out of here," Mrs. Pollifax pointed out. "We're supposed to be following the blue van, we have to catch up with Cyrus!"

He said gloomily, "I can scarcely help you look for this Cyrus if I am dead."

"But you're not dead," she reminded him matter-of-factly. "Why do they want to kill you, and who is *gawng john?*"

Bonchoo stirred, sighed and straightened his shoulders. "It means guerrilla band, robber gang, not a person." He stood up and looked around, removed his hat and scratched his head, revealing the fact that he was nearly bald, which gave him even more of a brigand look. "I do not like this," he announced.

"Nor do I," said Mrs. Pollifax. "We can't leave this—this hoodlum and his motorcycle here," she pointed out.

"No," he said, and they regarded each other measuringly. "You are not scared?"

"At the moment I'm more 'scared' for Cyrus," she told him. "Do you think, please, we could get to work now before they wake up?"

"Yes," he said, jammed his hat squarely back on his head and rose to his feet.

Together they lifted Yellow Shirt and half-carried, half-dragged him into the underbrush to place next to his companion. The motorcycle was wheeled into the jungle a little farther down the road, a handful of sand and leaves was dropped into its gas tank, and while Mrs. Pollifax waited for him in the cab Bonchoo carefully rearranged bent saplings and twisted palms to conceal their invasion of the forest.

"Feeling better?" she asked as he joined her.

He gave her a rueful smile. "I guess." Climbing in beside her he started the engine and they were off again.

But something had subtly changed between them: each of them had become slightly more of a person to the other now, bringing interesting new dimensions to their thinking. Having proceeded on the uneasy basis of appearances, and a need for expediency, they were now more aware of what lay behind the other's facades: Bonchoo had openly admitted to being afraid, which surprised her and rendered him less threatening, while Bonchoo was finding her not quite the stereotype of Helpless American that he'd assumed. Mrs. Pollifax found herself going back over the scene in the Chiang Mai hut and applying friendlier aspects to it: he might have killed Ruamsak but the fact that he had not abandoned her so far struck her now as an aspect of character rather than ominous. She thought that her instincts might have been sound after all when she had decided to accept Bonchoo and to continue on with him. Nevertheless it was becoming very important to break down his defenses soon and learn who the crafty *naga* might be who was behind the near-killing on the road. In the meantime she gazed thoughtfully out of the window at the road, at groves of bamboo rising in graceful columns, at a bald hilltop glimpsed in the distance that was planted with tiny new trees in rows like stripes of chenille across a brown cloth. A tiny bus charged down upon them at breakneck speed and was gone. Up ahead she saw a car that had stalled beside the edge of the road and she leaned forward, frowning. She said, "Bonchoo, isn't that—?" and then, "It's blue!" she cried. "Bonchoo, look—it's a van, a blue van!"

Bonchoo was already slowing the truck. "Yes!" he shouted back.

From a distance it looked as if the car had run off the road into a ditch, except there were no ditches along the road. It leaned crazily to one side as if an axle had broken, or a wheel had been lost but there it was, shabby, old and unmistakably blue. She felt a flare of excitement.

Bonchoo cautiously drove past the van and then turned around and drove back and parked behind it. "Empty," he said.

"Yes, but Cyrus could still be in the back," she told him. "If they've had to abandon the van and walk—" Her heart was singing. "They could scarcely take an unconscious man with them, could they? Wouldn't they have to walk?" Without waiting for a reply she flung open the door and was out of the truck and running, with Bonchoo hurrying behind her. She opened the van's door and peered inside. Her hopeful heart constricted: Cyrus was not inside, the rear was empty.

"He's not here," she said, tears rising in her eyes. "He's gone, they took him with them, but where?"

Bonchoo looked thoughtful. "I do not think they walk along this road if they have stolen a man, not with a police block half an hour from here." At her startled glance he said, "Oh yes, we are in the north now, where police set up barriers to check for smugglers and insurgents. So long as they drive in a car they would have a good story for the police, but to walk, with this Cyrus between them—" He shook his head.

"I wish you'd stop calling him 'this Cyrus,' " she said indignantly. "He was simply minding his own business, an innocent bystander carried off by unscrupulous people."

Bonchoo looked at her with interest. "Was he?" he said softly. "You know no reason for this kidnapping?"

"Certainly not," she said hotly.

He smiled a little. "You are crying."

"I'm not crying," she flung at him. "But if they didn't start walking along the road where would they go?"

Bonchoo's gaze shifted to the forest. "There," he said, and pointed.

She turned and looked at what he pointed: at the dense forest, and at level after level of dusty green rising beyond its edge. "There?" she said blankly. "But—that's jungle."

"There are trails."

"Where?"

"Not far if we are now less than one hour from Chiang Rai." He glanced up at the sun and then at the road and then at the shape of the hills around them. "Very near," he said, and strolling past the blue van he began examining the scrub along the shoulder of the road. "Here," he called out suddenly, pointing. "But not easy, it can be dangerous."

"If you think that's where they went then it's where I go, even by myself," she added defiantly.

He laughed. "You? By yourself? You'd be lost in an hour. Decide! Those two young *naklengs* will soon be sitting up and rubbing two sore heads."

"You mean you'll go too, Bonchoo? To—" She hesitated. "To gain merit?"

"I have much merit to earn," he said, nodding, but she thought he looked amused again. *"Much!* Okay we go, but first we hide these cars, too."

It proved impossible to move the blue van, even to roll it over, and so it was left where it stood by the side of the road, which pleased neither of them because it would be seen at once by the *naklengs.* Bonchoo's truck, however, was driven some distance down the road where it was carefully concealed behind a grove of bamboo trees and divested of eggs, bananas and colas, which they divided between their pockets and her purse.

Following this they approached the trail, leaving behind them —Mrs. Pollifax counted—one motorcycle, one truck, one blue van and two young men who might or might not be pursuing them soon.

"Here," Bonchoo said, showing her the path almost obscured from the road by scrub and bushes.

Mrs. Pollifax regarded it doubtfully; she'd not expected the trail to look so dark and forbidding, it was no more than a thread of tamped-down earth winding among towering trees and, worse, it soon slanted upward at a sharp angle. She glanced ruefully at the flimsy cotton shoes she'd chosen this morning, just because they matched her khaki slacks, and sighed over such vanity. Seeing a torn piece of paper next to her right shoe she automatically picked it up, glanced at it curiously and found herself staring in shock at a slip of paper on which was etched the blue eye of a fish —one eye, one fin—and under it the letters D-I-N-E-S.

"Sardines!" she cried. "Cyrus dropped this! Bonchoo, it's his!"

Bonchoo came to her side and looked at it, puzzled. "He dropped this? What is it? How can you know?"

"It's torn from a tin of sardines—he carried them in his camera bag—it's a message! This is where they went, and he's conscious and *alive!*"

"A very strange message," he said doubtfully.

"Trust me," she told him eagerly, and at once the narrow path no longer looked forbidding. "They haven't harmed him, he must be walking now, and this is where they went!"

"*Very* strange message," Bonchoo repeated, shaking his head.

Brushing aside dusty palm leaves and vines he held them back for her and with this they left behind the road to Chiang Rai and plunged into the jungle.

Chapter 7

It was a green and claustrophobic world they entered. Close to the road every leaf and stem was red with dust that rose in clouds as they passed; a few hundred feet inside and they left both dust and road behind them, as well as every evidence of civilization, so that only the thought of Cyrus passing this way steadied Mrs. Pollifax. The vegetation was dense: columns of trees climbed skyward, but at ground level scrub and scraggly new growth formed a wall on either side of the narrow trail, rising out of tangles of dried grass and palms and bamboo that struggled toward the sun. There was no sky: the foliage of the trees met and formed an arch overhead, turning the trail into a tunnel where only an occasional stripe of sunshine broke through to pattern the forest floor.

Bonchoo led the way. The stillness of the forest struck her at first as oppressive until a bird suddenly cried out overhead, and as it took flight she saw a flash of bright color high among the treetops. Leaves rustled and quivered at the bird's departure and then the forest became still again, but she felt a listening quality about it now, a sense of presences. As she trudged along behind Bonchoo she became aware that sometimes, far above them, trees stirred and leaves danced, and at such times a sweeter air drifted down to her but no breezes followed: on the forest floor it remained warm, humid, with a faint odor of earth and decaying roots.

"Are there snakes?" she called to Bonchoo.

She was becoming familiar now with his shrug. Over his shoulder he said, "Not so many as down on the plains, it's not as hot in the mountains. They come out only at night here."

It was a reply that was not entirely reassuring.

Occasionally the wall on either side thinned and if she removed her eyes from the trail, which increasingly hypnotized her, she saw clearings where a great tree had fallen, creating sun and space for new shoots of green to take root, where tiny white flowers grew over and around the fallen trunk. But presently her glance stopped wandering because they began to climb again, the path moving up toward the ridges that she'd seen from the road. Bonchoo was a fast walker: determined to keep up with him she tried not to notice that after half an hour she had begun to pant. She was also growing hungry and she was tiring but most of all she was thirsty. Stealing a glance at her watch she saw that it was nearing noon, which gave her hope that soon Bonchoo might halt his relentless pace and consider rest and some food.

Steadily they marched along until they emerged from woods into a clearing covered with tall imperata grass; they had reached the summit of this particular hill, and looking ahead she saw they must next walk downhill for perhaps half a mile and then climb to a still higher hill. She sighed. "Are there wild animals?"

He turned to her. "Not many. Deer, a few bears. You are afraid?" he asked, looking at her seriously.

"I just like to know what to expect," she told him, adding, "I'm thirsty, can we stop now?"

"When we reach the next ridge," he said, pointing. "There has been a fire there, as you can see, and we will be able to see ahead and behind us."

He meant, of course, that the two *naklengs* might already be following them but she did not care to think about that. She gave the ridge a hostile glance and fell into step behind Bonchoo again. Reentering the forest she caught a glimpse of another bril-

liant-plumaged bird and wondered if Cyrus might have seen it,
too, bird-watcher that he was, but it was not time to think of
Cyrus, either. She still held in her hand the slip of paper with the
fish eye and the letters D-I-N-E-S that was all of Cyrus that she
possessed now but she sternly told herself it would only sap her
flagging energy to go over and over why he had been abducted,
and what those people wanted of him, and having sternly told
herself not to think about this she at once began wondering why
he'd been abducted and what those people wanted of him, whoever they were . . .

Whoever they were . . . This was what she had to find out
from Bonchoo when they reached the next ridge and rested. Cyrus had been mysteriously carried off, Ruamsak was dead in
Chiang Mai and the only man who could explain any of this
strode along the trail in front of her, his own life apparently in
danger for reasons unknown to her. Presently—she glanced at
her watch again—the two men who had tried to kill Bonchoo
would have found the blue van parked at the side of the road and
if they remained determined to kill Bonchoo they would guess
where they had gone, and follow.

For just a moment, her tiredness bringing an odd detachment,
she saw herself and Bonchoo in pursuit of Cyrus somewhere
ahead of them, and the two *naklengs* possibly giving chase behind them, and here she was, Emily Reed-Pollifax, in a jungle in
northern Thailand, hurrying along behind a man she scarcely
knew. Her thoughts went back to a sunny kitchen and Bishop
saying, "It's a very small errand, just pick up a package for
us . . ." She was appalled at his naïvete and his miscalculations
angered her now, she admitted it.

But the horror of the situation, and what kept her trudging
after Bonchoo in spite of growing exhaustion was why Cyrus had
been taken, what they wanted of him and what they would do to
him when they learned he was of no use to them. And she did not
even know who "they" were, and such helplessness was always
enraging. She glanced up into the thick unruly wall of trees grop-
ing toward sky and sunlight and suddenly the forest seemed a

very sinister place to her. To watch the trail was kinder, and she lowered her eyes, shook her head, sighed, gritted her teeth and walked on, one step after another, feet hurting now, legs trembling from walking downhill and then uphill, and thirsty.

"Almost there," Bonchoo said.

She lifted her eyes: they had come out on the ridge and had reached the clearing which had begun greening over with soft tender grass.

"Slash-and-burn," Bonchoo told her. "A rice or poppy field once—for the hill people—until the earth grew tired." He led her across the field to its far edge and she sank down gratefully on a rock shaded by the forest ahead.

"Something to drink, please," she said.

He handed her a lukewarm cola. "Not too fast," he warned her. "We have two bottles left, and you—you being *farang* you must not drink water."

"It's lovely, it's so *wet,*" she said, licking her lips.

"We stop for fifteen minutes only. Eat," he said, and handed her a hard-boiled egg.

She was reviving; just to sit was glorious, and putting down the cola she began to peel the egg. Glancing at Bonchoo, seated cross-legged on the grass, she said, "It's time you talk, Bonchoo . . . those men wanted to kill you and I want to know why."

He nodded cheerfully. "Yes, and you chop-chopped the second one, which saved my life. I am grateful—much merit for you!"

"Grateful enough," she said dryly, "to explain this—this cast of characters I've been thrown among? I mean, all I did was walk into a hut with bougainvillea over its fence and now I've lost a husband, and here I am on a jungle hilltop with you."

He nodded judiciously. "That is true, yes . . . okay," he said, and thought a minute. "I will tell you a story."

"Yes, tell me a story," she urged.

He took a deep breath. "To begin, I live in Chiang Saen, where lives also my friend Ruamsak, who needed help from me."

She was careful not to react to his naming Ruamsak. "That's the town up on the border?" she asked coolly.

He nodded. "Yes. There is also this American there who calls himself Jacoby, which may or may not be his name."

"Jacoby," she repeated—*and Ruamsak,* she added to herself triumphantly, feeling that at last a connection was being made that she could understand.

"When there were Americans here," Bonchoo said, "this Jacoby came with the CIA but he got into drugs and when the Americans left Thailand in '76 he stayed. In Chiang Saen there are always drugs, you understand? Because in Mae Sai and Chiang Saen—well, that is the Golden Triangle, as it is called. So he stayed there in a guesthouse."

She nodded and watched him efficiently slice his egg with the murder knife.

"But this Jacoby," he went on, "would still pass information to his CIA people in the U.S.A. Drugs are cheap in Chiang Saen when a man is not a drug agent and can be trusted, but drugs still need money to buy. Sometimes, with my connections, I would hear things and tell Jacoby; I would earn some *baht* from him in that way and he would earn some U.S. dollars for his opium. He still had that U.S. connection—I knew about that, when he was smoking opium he would boast of it to me."

Bonchoo sighed. "It is important never to trust people who smoke opium, this I know, so I was very careful. I did not trust Jacoby, I did not trust the few friends he had, I only trusted his *baht.*"

"Very sensible," agreed Mrs. Pollifax.

He shrugged. "So when my friend Ruamsak comes to me to ask how he can sell big information he has—big political information—I ask myself how this could be delivered without Jacoby taking all the money. But only Jacoby knows what to do, so finally I have to go to him and speak of Ruamsak; I tell him Ruamsak will share money but not information, which is political in nature. Of course Jacoby tries to find out who Ruamsak is and what he knows but this I refuse." He stopped and added very seriously, "It had something to do with a coup planned soon in my country."

"Oh," said Mrs. Pollifax, startled. "But—how would this Ruamsak know?"

"Because Ruamsak travels many places," said Bonchoo solemnly.

"Why?" asked Mrs. Pollifax. "How?"

"He is a smuggler. He is a smuggler of teak."

"Of *what?*"

"Oh yes. Teak is not legal to cut now in my country, there are laws against it, the government is busy with programs to grow new teak before it's all gone. So Ruamsak goes into Burma—" He pointed toward the mountain range behind them. "He buys teak logs and floats them down the Mekong at night to sell on the black market. When he goes back into Burma he takes spare auto parts, lipsticks, radios, flashlights. Sometimes he smuggles things across the Mekong into Laos, too—he goes many places and hears many things."

"All right, I understand," she said, nodding.

"So Ruamsak I trust but not Jacoby. Jacoby makes arrangements, he tells me Ruamsak is to go to Chiang Mai to meet a person who will come to him there. I am suspicious and decide I follow my friend Ruamsak to make sure it's all okay."

He leaned forward, waving his knife. "And I am wise to not trust Jacoby, you see how he betrays Ruamsak. He sets a trap to kill him. Jacoby is in very bad shape from his opium smoking so I think he turned to the only people he knows now: the men he buys his drugs from." Bonchoo shivered. "Wen Sa's men."

Mrs. Pollifax, about to bite into an egg, paused.

"And who is Wen Sa?"

Bonchoo lowered his voice. "Please, it is not a name to speak loudly. He is general of the biggest rebel army in Burma, a Shan warlord. He also controls most of the opium trade, a dangerous man. They say he comes often into this country in disguise, just comes and goes."

Astonished, she said, "But if he's that big, why on earth would he pay any attention to Jacoby? Why should he help an American who's a drug addict?"

Bonchoo scowled. "I think and think about this since we left Chiang Mai. He would help Jacoby only if Jacoby told him something clever and sly. I think Jacoby must have lied to him and told Wen Sa's men that Ruamsak learned where opium refineries are hidden in the jungle . . . Americans are very interested in this; your people spend millions to help the Thai police stamp out opium. Why else would Wen Sa's men follow Ruamsak to Chiang Mai and kill him? They are not interested in political information."

Mrs. Pollifax frowned. "So it was one of Wen Sa's men who killed Ruamsak in the hut?"

"He was very dead," pointed out Bonchoo. "With a Shan knife in him, and as you know they sent a number of men to be sure the job was done. The blue van. The two *naklengs* on the motorcycle. There is much determination there!"

"Yes, and kidnapped Cyrus as well," she reminded him. She studied his broad, high-cheekboned face, trying to sort out the facts he had given her and to weigh them. This was not New York or even Bangkok, she thought dryly, it was a very strange world to her; she was not accustomed to warlords and smugglers and it was necessary to translate his story into something she could understand, to forget that she was seated in a hilltop jungle and to reduce Bonchoo's story to facts, understandable facts. And the longer she thought about what he had told her the less satisfied she became: there was something wrong, it was too complicated and it did not match what she knew of human nature.

There were too many people in his story.

She said idly, "And you insist that Ruamsak's information had nothing at all to do with this Wen Sa and his—uh—opium empire?"

Bonchoo said firmly, "Absolutely. Ruamsak I trust."

She nodded, and having gone over his story again a twinkle came into her eyes and she smiled. "You know, Bonchoo," she said, "you make an excellent storyteller but I don't believe your story. If I'd not been so worried about Cyrus—"

Affronted, he said, "You call me a liar!"

She shook her head. "Oh no, but a very good teller of tales, except that your story simply doesn't add up."

"Add up?" He scowled at her. "Why? How?"

She held up one hand, and finger by finger ticked off the discrepancies. "One, if you didn't trust Jacoby you would scarcely have gone to him and placed Ruamsak's life in his hands. Two, after doing that you allowed Ruamsak to go to Chiang Mai and then you followed only to see if it was a trap. Three, you were there in the hut with the dead man and you certainly didn't act as if a good friend of yours had been murdered, and four, if you're not involved in all this, why did those two men try to kill you on the road?" She sat back, smiling at him. "As I say, if I'd not been so upset about Cyrus I'd have realized at once that Ruamsak wasn't killed in that hut in Chiang Mai."

"But you saw him dead!" he protested.

She shook her head. "I saw someone dead but I don't believe at all in your Ruamsak; I don't, for instance, believe he's dead at all. I think Ruamsak is very much alive and it was someone else who was killed back there in the hut."

His mouth dropped open. "Not Ruamsak!"

"No," she said smiling at him, "because I think I am sitting here and eating eggs with Ruamsak and I've been traveling with him all this time." Pointing a finger at him she said, *"You're* Ruamsak."

His eyes narrowed. There was silence while they regarded each other warily, a silence long enough for her to realize that if Bonchoo preferred not to be identified as Ruamsak he could easily kill her and dispose of her right now.

But she had misjudged him, it was his pride that had been wounded, as she realized when he lifted a hand and hit himself on the forehead, a gesture both despairing and oddly touching. *"Yai,* but I am no damn good at this game," he said sorrowfully. "Yes I am Ruamsak. But Ruamsak is only a name, the name of my grandfather. I did not lie, I am really Bonchoo, you understand."

She smiled. "Then I'm terribly glad to meet you at last—both you and Ruamsak—because I thought I'd lost not only Cyrus but Ruamsak. You see, I didn't just wander into that alley to take snapshots, Cyrus and I were the ones sent to meet Ruamsak and pick up his package of information."

He startled her by bursting into laughter. "This is so? I ask you," he said, "who would have thought it? They send me a clever one! I thought maybe it could be your husband but it is true that after seeing you back there—" He lifted an arm and slashed at the air.

"Cyrus is very clever, too," she told him primly, "but if you're Ruamsak then where is the information you were to give us?"

He stopped laughing. "It didn't occur to you?" he said in surprise.

"What didn't occur?"

"Your husband must have the package, or why else would they have seized him and taken him away?"

Chapter 8

"Cyrus?" she gasped. "How could Cyrus possibly have it? He was captured out on the street, he didn't even enter the alley!"

Behind them in the jungle a parrot gave a fierce derisive squawk that was answered from a tall tree to their left. "Don't throw those eggshells," Bonchoo said quickly, "they would be noticed by anyone behind us."

"Bonchoo," she repeated sharply, "how could Cyrus possibly have your package?"

He sighed. "Very easily, I am sad to say. You must understand what I had was a letter to hide. The information I carry in my head but of what use without proof, who would believe? It had to be hidden cleverly so I took it yesterday to a man in a lacquer shop to have it made into a *phyot* arm-ring, which wards off evil spirits." He explained to her how he had rolled the letter into a tube, and what the man had told him. "It's too bad the lac needed time for drying; I should have thought of something else but it was too late. He was to bring it to me this morning, early. Before you came I was hiding outside the window, trying to think what to do next, when someone rushed into the hut, gave a cry and ran out." He lifted both hands in a gesture that was both rueful and apologetic. "I think it was the man delivering the arm-ring, I think it had to be."

She thought back to a more carefree hour of the day. "Someone did run out of the alley," she said slowly. "I'd forgotten that, he nearly ran into me. He was certainly in a great hurry."

Bonchoo sighed. "Can there be any other reason your husband was taken away? The man from the lacquer shop came to deliver my arm-ring; he found a dead man and rushed out. In a panic the man must have dropped the arm-ring and your husband picked it up, or even maybe he gave it to him, anything to be rid of it." He added thoughtfully, "You notice the men did not kidnap the man from the lacquer shop, it was your Cyrus they chose."

She frowned over this. "You mean they were across the street watching and waiting?"

"Yes, waiting for the man who tried to kill me to come out and say I am dead. And for him to bring with him the package they had been told I had."

"I must have proved rather useful, then, as a shield." She reflected that the hut had certainly been a busy place for that hour, and she winced as she remembered how casually she had walked down that alley. She said, "It was you who killed the Shan in the hut, then."

He nodded. "Yes, and for such a matter I lose great merit, even if it is to save my own life. We fought hard, he was very strong." He shivered. "I have never killed a man before, this is a grave matter for a Buddhist."

She said soberly, "But you're earning back much merit by your kindness in helping me now."

"Kindness!" he exploded. "You think I can go back to my family and to my village when Wen Sa's men think I am informer?" His hand darted to his throat and with a finger he slashed it from left to right. "Nobody is safe from Wen Sa's men when it's believed he's a spy. No, it's not kindness. I have no future, I am not safe until I find the *phyot*-ring and prove Jacoby is a big liar."

"You hope to find Wen Sa, then?"

"Nobody finds Wen Sa," he told her, "but I know many of his men, our paths cross in the mountains, all of us being smugglers—"

"So you really are a teak smuggler," she broke in.

He nodded. "—and they will take my words to him. I told you I know them." His lips tightened. "This Jacoby is a snake, I tell you, a *naga.*"

She looked at him curiously, again seeing him differently. "How on earth did you become involved in this?" she asked. "How on earth did you ever contact people in the—well, the United States?"

"Oh, I wrote letter to them," he said simply.

She stared at him in astonishment. "You *wrote* to them, you simply wrote a *letter?*"

"Of course. Jacoby was all the time smoking opium . . . I grow suspicious how he earns so much U.S. money to buy it when he pays so little *baht* to me for the gossip I bring him. One day I sneak a look in the steel box in his room, and just as I suspect, everything he is paid for is what I, Bonchoo, pass on to him. I am earning all his money for him!

"But there was more," he said. "He had made certain changes in what I tell him, he was sending lies." He shook his head. "Jacoby was—how you say—playing two games against a middle, working for the Vietnamese across the river in Laos, too. And the address I found there, a Mr. James T. Carstairs—"

"In Baltimore, Maryland," she said with a smile, nodding.

"Yes, so I write to this Mr. Carstairs, I offer a deal. I tell them if interested they can write to me—but I took such care," he said, scowling. "I was so careful! They wrote to me in care of the jade shop in Mae Sai which my *hnawng kuhee*—brother-in-law— owns. That was a few months ago, and that is how it began."

"I don't know why I'm surprised," she said contritely. "I myself applied in person for work as a spy. You hoped to make money doing this?"

He sighed. "I smuggle teak but when I tell you I have five children, a wife, a mother-in-law, a father-in-law living in my house you will understand there is never enough money, not with all the bribes I have to pay the patrols. I was greedy," he said sadly. "But I was also very careful, so I do not understand. Jacoby must have seen me going through his papers—I don't know —or maybe when I stopped coming to him with news he turned sly and paid someone to follow me and learn why. I have not been careful enough, I see this," he said ruefully.

"Did Jacoby come to Chiang Mai? Was he one of the men in the blue van?"

"Oh no, Jacoby is too sick to walk far, he could never leave Chiang Saen."

"And you really believe he turned to Wen Sa's men!"

Bonchoo shrugged. "In my village, where else could he turn, who else would he know? There are many Shan in my country, and they are peaceful. The man who tried to kill me was a Shan, and he was not peaceful. It was very well planned, too, and Thai people are not such good planners."

"How can you be so sure?" she asked curiously.

He smiled. "To you we look all alike, eh? I, for instance, am not pure Thai, I am half Chinese—a Thai-Chinese person. The hill-tribe people have Tibetan blood and dress like Laotians. The Vietnamese are tall. A Shan does not have to wear a towel wrapped around his head like a turban for me to know he's a Shan, it's in his face. But we have stopped long enough," he told her, with a glance at the position of the sun. "We've rested long enough, it's time to go."

Mrs. Pollifax nodded and stood up, stuffing banana skins and eggshells into her pocket. She had not been relieved of her worries about Cyrus but she could admit to relief at learning that Bonchoo was as motivated as she was in finding him. She would have liked to ask him about the political information that he carried in his head but that would have to wait for the next rest. She also longed to ask him what he thought of Cyrus' chances in the hands of Wen Sa's men but she needed very much just now to hang on to both optimism and hope and she wasn't sure that Bonchoo could provide either.

As if sensing her thoughts he gave her a sympathetic glance. "I want you to know, Mrs. Emily, if your *sahmee*—your husband I mean—has the *phyot* arm-ring with him he will be safe, I promise you, because it also contains a yantra blessed by the abbot of Chiang Rai."

Mrs. Pollifax was not entirely consoled by this but she thought that the blessings of a Chiang Rai abbot were not to be underestimated, and that it was generous of Bonchoo to tell her this.

"One thing more," he added as they prepared to leave. "We move very quietly now, this mountain country is dangerous. No speaking!"

Startled, she said, "Dangerous how? Wen Sa's men?"

He shook his head. "Bandits."

"Bandits?"

"Like the snakes they come out mostly at night but if they hear or see us, and you an American—"

Nothing had prepared her for bandits. "But who are *they?*" she gasped.

"Thai *naklengs* too lazy to work," he said scornfully. "They rob the hill tribes who have no protection, they prey on them like vultures and rob anybody else they find who walks on the trails with no gun. We do not have a gun," he pointed out.

Mrs. Pollifax thought of the cube of pure gold that she carried in her purse. "You mean we must beware of bandits as well as Wen Sa's men?"

"And of the hill-tribe people who might think we are bandits."

"Might think we are bandits," she repeated dazedly.

He added comfortingly, "It's fortunate that you are a woman, and American; I do not think any opium smugglers will think you a spy and kill you. You do not look a spy at all," he told her happily, his face beaming at having found such reassurance for her.

"How nice," she said weakly. "This is certainly very different from Bangkok!"

"Oh—Bangkok," he said dismissingly. "Bangkok is only big showcase. Bangkok sucks the rest of the country dry, it grows rich and big while people in the north grow poorer and poorer. *Nothing* changes here—nothing!"

His anger startled her but she said nothing; quiet she would be, and slinging her purse over her shoulder she tucked the remainder of the precious cola in her pocket and followed him into the dark opening where the trail resumed. They had left no traces of their stop; Bonchoo had even coaxed the grass upright where he'd sat. She was beginning to understand the importance of this as the surrounding forest changed again for her, no longer a deserted and mountainous corner of the north but a place where people pursued dangerous games, followed secret trails, moved across borders, made their own rules and killed or robbed intruders.

Oh, Bishop, she thought reproachfully, and then, *Oh Cyrus,* and she was aware again of how a life could change in the flick of an eyelash, or at a pause beside a water jug in Chiang Mai. On the positive side, however—and she had grown tired of dark thoughts—she had not left a dead Ruamsak behind her after all, and she had her fragment of sardine wrapper to prove that Cyrus had been alive when he entered the jungle. She thought also—not without grim humor—that this was certainly an interesting way to distance herself from the Hong Kong experience; there was nothing quite like the prospect of facing bandits, opium smugglers and hill-tribe people to exorcise an experience in the past. It was reassuring, too, to learn that Bonchoo had a wife and family in Chiang Saen: links of dependency were being forged between them that she hoped would not unravel as they traveled on.

Or as she tired . . . there was that, certainly, because Bonchoo was strong, he was a man accustomed to steep mountain trails and to roping together such huge logs of teak as she had seen pass by when she sat on the terrace of the hotel in Bangkok. Since her experience in Hong Kong—*say it, Emily,* she told herself, *you were tortured*—she had been something of a convalescent, still doing her yoga and practicing her karate but—she had to admit this, too—allowing Cyrus to pamper her. She was out of condition when she could least afford to be, and if those two young *naklengs,* as Bonchoo called them, were on the trail behind them now . . . She did not finish the thought. She had just lifted her eyes to what lay ahead, and as her eyes followed a trail that met the side of a mountain and went up—and then up higher still—she thought in horror, *Good God, it's like a ski trail.*

Whether she was in condition or not she understood that she was going to have to push herself mercilessly and pick up the pieces later; there would be time enough to relax once they found Cyrus.

If we find him, she thought bleakly . . . if we *can* . . . and discovered that her thoughts were darkening again. She glanced at her watch: time had stopped existing for her but she saw that the time lacked fifteen minutes to two o'clock and they had therefore been climbing up and down these tortuous trails for three hours.

Courage, Emily, she told herself, and drawing a deep breath began to climb the hill.

An hour later, stumbling along behind Bonchoo, Mrs. Pollifax realized that she was nursing a blister on her right heel, as well as a blister on the sole of her left foot. She wondered how many miles they'd walked since they entered the jungle but this scarcely seemed relevant when so much of it had been uphill. Irrationally, even crossly, she found herself remembering her former neighbor Miss Hartshorne, who planned her annual tours around cathedrals and museums and tirelessly photographed them for slides to view with her neighbors once at home. Mrs. Pollifax, wiping sweat from her forehead, wondered what Miss Hartshorne would think if she could see her now, limping along a forest trail, bedraggled, blistered and sweaty, lacking official guides and historic buildings. It was a pity, she thought, that Miss Hartshorne had never known where she went when she vanished periodically to work for Carstairs; Mrs. Pollifax had often been accused by her friend of lacking a sense of adventure, and—later—that she chose such unpleasant places with which to begin her travels, a view shared by her daughter Jane. *"Bulgaria?"* Jane had wailed. "Mother, how can you choose such an inconvenient place!"

Jane, she felt, would consider this too an inconvenient place. In fact only her son Roger had ever suspected anything unorthodox behind her sudden departures. It was her son Roger who had told Cyrus with a grin, "I can't tell you how relieved I am to see her marrying you. Those weird trips she's taken, with never a postcard from her and never any photographs of what she's seen, not to mention her return from Switzerland with her arm in a sling, and from China with a broken wrist, and the most improbable explanations!"

"Turning her over to me, are you?" Cyrus had asked with a twinkle.

"Gladly," Roger had said with feeling. "I suspect you know very well what she's been up to but I've never wanted to pry. Now *you* can do the worrying."

These thoughts only barely diverted her as she limped along behind Bonchoo. *Mind over matter,* she told herself, determined not to collapse until Bonchoo did, and having finished that particular train of thought she turned to exercising her fingers for coin palming, and tried not to notice that the blister on her heel had just broken and that it was probably blood that was seeping into her shoe.

The trail had narrowed, and if they were now several thousand feet above sea level they were also closer to the sun. The accumulated heat of the day had turned the air in the forest oppressive and still. Into this stillness there came a faint rustle among the tangles beside the trail, as if a small and very welcome breeze stirred the leaves.

Bonchoo suddenly stopped. Staring into the underbrush he raised both hands and shouted, *"Rau penn ploen—rau penn ploen!"*

Disconcerted, Mrs. Pollifax stopped, too, and looked into the forest, seeing nothing at first, and then in the dim light her glance caught the gleam of something long and thin and metallic protruding from the leaves. She thought, *That's a rifle,* and she stood very still.

A harsh voice called back, *"Rau penn kai?"*

Bonchoo began speaking rapidly, lightly, with many shrugs and a wry note in his voice. The tangles parted: the rifle emerged first and then the man, small and wiry, his brown face a network of lines like seams stitching together features that looked almost Tibetan, the cheekbones so high they nearly suffocated his bright and wary eyes. He wore a rusty black shirt, gray pants, sandals and a band of ragged cotton around his head. From one shoulder hung a game bag and from his waist a machete in a sheath made of reed.

She said anxiously, "What is he saying?"

"I've told him we're friends."

"Yes but does he believe you?"

Bonchoo said dryly, "If he believed me he would remove the rifle from my stomach."

"But who is he?"

"He's an Akha and he doesn't speak Thai very well. He insists we go with him to his village to see the headman, who does speak Thai. It's about three kilometers from here."

"But I don't want to go!" she protested.

"No? We're lucky he didn't shoot first," Bonchoo said. "Apparently there's been some trouble here this week. If I can just convince the headman we're not spies or bandits—"

"I don't feel at all like a bandit, I just feel tired," she said crossly. "Ask him if he's seen a very large American with two Shan."

Bonchoo shook his head. "Later, later. Think you can manage three more kilometers?"

"Uphill or down?"

He smiled reluctantly. "The Akha never live on hilltops so it will be halfway down the mountain. Maybe half up, half down."

She sighed. "Let's get it over with then," and wondered why the Akha never lived on the mountaintops.

This time the Akha led the way, which surprised Mrs. Pollifax because she thought that, if either she or Bonchoo had the energy, they could easily overpower him from the rear. This delusion was dismissed, however, when she clumsily stepped on a dry branch that had fallen across the trail: the man whirled and this time it was she who felt the rifle pressed into her stomach. She gave the man a weak, apologetic smile and they continued.

She was beginning to feel lightheaded from altitude and exhaustion when the Akha stopped and held up a hand, listening. Turning, he gave them each a hard glance and spoke in a low voice to Bonchoo.

"We leave the trail," Bonchoo told her. "Fast! And don't speak!"

Stepping under and over vines and scrub, pushing aside long sweeping branches and tall razor grass, she followed the two men off the trail into the jungle. Mercifully they did not have to go far; reaching a screen of palms they simply stood, Mrs. Pollifax wondering what on earth was happening until, very faintly, she heard a soft plodding of hoofs. Off to her right a cloud of dust drifted in among the trees, and then—on a trail that ran counter to theirs, and no more than twenty feet in front of them—a procession of donkeys began passing their hiding place in a long line, each bearing loaded panniers, the procession led by a man wearing a dusty turban and carrying a stick. He was followed by three other men walking stolidly, silently along the forest trail with no whisper of sound except for the muted thud-thud of the animals' hoofs and a faint creak of leather. It was the silence of their passing that awed her, they seemed to her to be moving in and out of her vision like figures in a dream.

The dream and the silence were abruptly shattered by shouts behind the caravan. The procession came to a stop and two men hurried up the trail, calling and waving to them.

Bonchoo nudged Mrs. Pollifax and she nodded: one of the young men wore a bright red shirt and the other a bright yellow shirt: she recognized them both.

So they're still after us, she thought bleakly, *and what astonishingly fast time they've made! I didn't hit Yellow Shirt hard enough,* she thought sadly, and deplored her lack of ruthlessness. She could see the faces of the two clearly now through the screen of leaves as they talked and gestured to the men of the caravan. Red Shirt was very young but he looked tense as a coiled spring, face intent, eyes narrowed as he spoke. His companion in the yellow shirt looked less ambitious but less innocent as well: he had a hungry, wolflike face. Something was decided, the four men of the caravan did not look pleased but they nodded and the procession resumed its pace with Red Shirt and Yellow Shirt following in the rear.

In their hiding place they waited for a long time, which gave Mrs. Pollifax far too many minutes to understand that the two young *naklengs* had not abandoned their hunt but were working the trails now looking for them, and if the path they had taken was a shorter one, as it had to be, then it meant that they knew the jungle very well. She thought, *They must not find Bonchoo.* He was her lifeline, he was all that stood between her and the forest's unknowns . . . She decided fiercely that she must not, *would* not, allow those two hoodlums to kill him.

The sounds of the caravan had been gone for some ten minutes before the Akha moved. Leading them across the broader trail he pushed aside palms and scrub and they entered a footpath that was no more than a thread of a trail, scarcely visible and nearly overgrown.

To Bonchoo she said in a low voice, "Did the two *naklengs* ask those men if they'd seen us?"

He nodded. "Yes, and they came very near to seeing us, too, for which I will burn much incense at the temple—if I live through all this."

"And the caravan, was that opium?"

"No, no . . . guns."

"I'm so tired, Bonchoo. And thirsty."

"Another mile," he told her.

Another mile . . . her feet felt to her like bleeding stumps and her horizons had shrunken now to a thin line of red earth on the path in front of her; any future beyond the next moment was beyond comprehension, and the hope of catching up with Cyrus was receding into a distant dream that lay beyond a tougher goal called Survival: surviving collapse, thirst, two young *naklengs* searching for them, and now this detour to a mysterious village where a mysterious headman would decide if they were dangerous. Time blurred; she counted the pebbles on the path and tried to breathe deeply, which was easier now because the trail had leveled and the endless climbing had ceased. But still the mile that Bonchoo had promised her felt like an eternity.

Somewhere ahead a dog barked. In the woods a pig grunted. She looked up from counting pebbles and saw a clearing ahead of them, saw the outline of a steep thatched roof and then a dusty compound with a pig scratching in the earth. The path broadened, they entered the compound and the scene was no longer empty as people came into view: half a dozen children came racing toward them, followed more slowly by women in strange, cone-shaped headdresses, the women holding back shyly.

"We're here," Bonchoo said, and then, seeing her face he said anxiously, "Are you all right?"

She looked at him and then at the sunbaked clearing, gold in the afternoon sun. She said in a trembling voice, "If I could just —" She stopped and began again. "If I could just—"

The words refused to come; she stared at Bonchoo and at the Akha in astonishment, gasped and fell forward. The two men caught her just before she hit the ground.

Chapter 9

The news of a coup underway in Thailand reached Carstairs at seven o'clock Thursday evening and he realized that still another evening would be devoted to affairs in Bangkok. The coup had begun an hour earlier with the capture of Radio Thailand, and it was rumored that First Army Headquarters in the heart of the city had been surrounded and captured. Eleven people were reported dead and thirty-six wounded. According to the meager news given to the U.S. Embassy and the wire services, the coup attempt involved rebel forces in the Thai Army, but led by whom was unknown. The coup had begun at six o'clock on Friday morning.

In Langley, Virginia, it was still Thursday.

"Really spooky, these time differences," Bishop ventured as he returned to his desk to analyze the information reaching them. "Positively mystical, realizing that right now, at this very moment—" He glanced at his watch. "At this very moment it's 7:20 Friday morning over there and people already know what Friday's like, and have also," he added pointedly, "had a charming sleep tonight, which you and I may be denied, and they're actually experiencing a day we've not reached yet."

"You're being whimsical," growled Carstairs.

"No, I suspect rather metaphysical," Bishop said, considering this. "Fraught with time-and-space speculations, surely? Do you think, by the way, that Mornajay's mysterious flight to Bangkok had anything to do with this coup?"

Carstairs said with a wry smile, "The department provides no crystal balls, unfortunately. Of course anything's possible but if news of a pending coup drew him there then everyone Upstairs would know where he was, and above all his assistant. No, my best instincts tell me that something else is afoot."

"Are you thinking this because of his insistence on using a novice like McAndrews?"

Carstairs looked troubled. "That, too, is completely out of character for the very efficient Mornajay, but so is his bolting and leaving so many stones unturned."

"With the possibility of nasty things under those stones?" suggested Bishop. "There—I've said it. I know you swear at him a lot but what's your impression of the man?"

"A cold and uncomfortable person, all brain and no heart," Carstairs said. "Comes from cold country too—Minneapolis. You heard Holloway describe him: a large man with a large ego to match."

Bishop shook his head. *"Very* mysterious, although I have to confess that what worries me most about this coup are the eleven people reported dead, and thirty-six injured, and McAndrews still hasn't turned up a clue as to where Emily and Cyrus might be."

Carstairs said briskly, "Nonsense, they'd scarcely be—" He stopped, looking startled.

"Ah, but we don't know where they are, do we?" said Bishop pleasantly. "Dare I remind you of the many times you believed Mrs. Pollifax to be somewhere she wasn't? A few years ago you thought she was stuck in Istanbul and she turned up in prison halfway across the country in Kayseri. You were sure she was in Bulgaria and she telephoned us from Switzerland. You thought her dead in Mexico and she turned up bobbing along in a boat on the Adriatic, so how can you say they're not in Bangkok? Damn it," he said impatiently, "it's been hours since we notified the U.S. Embassy they're missing. Where are they, and why don't we hear from someone?"

"Patience, Bishop," said Carstairs. "It's only morning there, people have been sleeping."

Bishop yawned. "Lucky them." The telex began clicking again and Bishop leaned over it. "It says 'extremely fluid situation . . .' "

"That ubiquitous phrase that means they don't know what the hell's going on," Carstairs said with a sigh. "Whether right-wing fanatics are behind this, liberals, an old power elite or a new one, and above all whether they're pro or anti-American and will succeed or fail."

"Wait, there's more," Bishop told him. "No Americans killed —that's a relief, sorry as I am about the others. Ah—here we are —the coup is now rumored to be led by a General Lueng Nuang."

"Files," Carstairs said quickly. "He should be there. If not, try the computer."

"Right." As he walked past the phone he saw its red light flashing and plucked it from its nest, saying "Carstairs' office . . ." He handed the phone to Carstairs. "It's Mornajay's assistant, Mrs. Hudson."

"Good—I told her I'd like to interview Mornajay's appointment Monday morning at the time of the phone call from Bangkok; he or she may have overheard something helpful . . . Yes, Mrs. Hudson," he said, and turned silent, listening closely.

Bishop, curious, gave him sidelong glances as he searched for a file on General Lueng. When Carstairs did speak again Bishop jumped.

"Who?" he said in a startled voice, and began scribbling notes. When he'd thanked Mrs. Hudson he dialed a number and asked to speak to a man named Lester Thomson.

Bishop found two paragraphs in the files on General Lueng and extracted them to read. He noted that the general had been a member of the Thai Parliament eight years ago, until it had been discovered that his personal fortune had ballooned to five million Thai dollars due to bribes and to payoffs in drug smuggling. Reading between the lines Bishop gathered that several others in high positions had also been involved, but that General Lueng had been made an example of to please the Americans, who were still investing thousands in helping to root out the drug trade. General Lueng had languished in prison for all of three months, had then been exiled out of the country and had returned within a year to become a general in the army again, from which Bishop concluded dryly that there was a deficiency of generals in the country, and that the old-boy system was alive and flourishing. While he scanned the material he could hear Carstairs introducing himself on the phone to Thomson and asking if he could see him as soon as possible.

"He's coming right over," Carstairs told Bishop, the call ended.

"But who is he?"

A wicked little smile hovered on Carstairs' lips. "Would you believe he's DEA?"

"Drug Enforcement Agency?" Bishop was astonished. *"That* was Mornajay's appointment on Monday?" It was not unusual for the various intelligence agencies to share information but technically such give-and-take was supposed to be authorized by Upstairs. Then he remembered that Mornajay *was* Upstairs, one of the top elite and presumably answerable to no one.

Thomson was prompt: a bulky man with Irish-blue eyes and a shrewd, humorous face. "You caught me just as I was leaving my office," he said. "You say this has something to do with my appointment on Monday with Mornajay?"

Carstairs nodded. "Yes."

There was silence while the two men eyed each other speculatively, and then Thomson said without expression, "He walked out in the middle of our appointment, and I've been trying to reach him ever since. His assistant has been extremely evasive when I've called, telling me he'll return my call, except he doesn't."

"You were seeing him on a matter of importance?"

"Top level importance—to Mornajay," said Thomson.

They're fencing—Thomson knows something, thought Bishop, and waited.

Carstairs said softly, "His assistant Mrs. Hudson has not been frank with you. Understandably, given the situation. Actually you seem to be the last person to have seen Mornajay, he's disappeared."

"Disappeared!"

"Apparently due to a mysterious phone call that came through while you were there."

Thomson shook his head. "Not necessarily."

Carstairs regarded him with interest. "Care to explain that? You said you were there on a matter of top level importance to *Mornajay?*"

Thomson brought out a cigarette and became very busy lighting it. When he put away his lighter he leaned back in his chair and crossed his legs. "All right, I'll level with you, but strictly off the record."

"Agreed," said Carstairs.

"Frankly, I feel I've been sitting on dynamite and I'm not sure how to handle it. I came to see Mornajay first thing on Monday to present him with certain facts we'd learned after months of undercover work. I wanted him to explain certain coincidences—"

Carstairs' brows rose. "Coincidences?"

Thomson stirred restlessly. "I'd feel better about telling this if I'd been able to finish my conversation with Mornajay. As it is, I'd only begun to sketch out the facts I'd brought him when he had a phone call and cut short our appointment. Very coldly and very curtly. Doesn't *anyone* know where he is?"

Carstairs studied him carefully. "I appreciate your candor," he said. "I think I can be equally as candid. Would it interest you to know—and this too is off the record—that after a number of phone calls we've established the fact that Mornajay's been seen in Thailand?"

Thomson said quietly, "That shocks me."

"Can you tell us why?"

Thomson sighed. "Okay, I'll sketch it in . . . As you know, the DEA is particularly active in Thailand, where we're doing our level best to help the government stamp out the drug racket, which I might add is at times like a finger in the proverbial dyke. We keep track of the various warlords with their private armies and the Chinese go-betweens and merchants, and so on."

"The *chiu chao?*" inquired Carstairs.

Thomson nodded. "They're involved, yes—that network of unions and guilds that goes back centuries to ancient China, the same network that put Chiang Khai-shek in power in China . . . Unfortunately when Mao took over China the *chiu chao* simply filtered out into Hong Kong, Macao, San Francisco and so on. A very closed group with enormous influence. Their banks—oh, they're very respectable now—are involved in laundering drug money, and for over a year now we've also known that one of their top men is non-Chinese, and an American."

Carstairs said incredulously, *"American?* With the *chiu chao?* Impossible, they'd never permit it."

Thomson said tersely, "He married into it—a woman named Chin-Ling."

Bishop froze. It needed all of his discipline to keep from giving Carstairs the quick sidelong glance that would betray to Thomson that the name was not unfamiliar.

Carstairs said evenly, "Go on . . ."

"We've called this chap Mr. X, because in certain—er—wiretapping episodes, that's how *they* refer to him. Very few people have ever seen him, he seems to operate mainly by telephone and by cable and to supply information and move large sums of money for them. He's very clever, very organized.

"But three weeks ago," he continued, "we lucked into something: one of their chaps was odd man out in an inside power play, and he had very strong suspicions that he was being poisoned. He came to us and turned informant."

Bishop waited, his mouth open, a strange feeling gripping him.

"He was in a position to give us something of a report on Mr. X," went on Thomson slowly. "He told us, for instance, that Mr. X knew Southeast Asia very well, having spent some years there during the Vietnam War, that he has apartments in Hong Kong and Bangkok, supports a wife in Bangkok but is seldom in either place. He uses the names Charlie Tegner and Kenneth Lance but his real name is Mornajay, first name unknown. He's about forty-five, was born in Minneapolis and it was during his stay in Asia during the war that he met and married this little Chinese girl named Chin-Ling, who just happened to have very high connections in the *chiu chao.*"

Bishop closed his mouth with a snap. It was happening, he was hearing it and it was incredible.

Carstairs said pleasantly, "And you have discovered that Mornajay here at CIA was in Vietnam during the war, is roughly forty-five or forty-seven, was born in Minneapolis and by curious coincidence his first name is Lance."

"Yes," said Thomson uncomfortably. "Another embarrassment for the CIA?"

There was silence and then Carstairs said smoothly, not acknowledging the hit, "Your appointment was interrupted by a phone call. Any idea who from?"

Thomson shook his head. "No, he took the call in an adjoining room behind a closed door."

Carstairs said nothing. *Aha,* thought Bishop, he's *not going to share what he knows about the call being from Chin-Ling.*

"And you really think," said Carstairs quietly, "that Mornajay could be your Mr. X?"

Thomson sighed. "I don't know, and he's in such a formidable position of authority that it's a hell of a responsibility, this. I'd feel happier about it if he'd been given the chance to deny it. Or explain it. Instead he's apparently just—bolted?"

Carstairs nodded. "The worst possible thing he could do."

"Have you told them Upstairs that he's in Thailand?"

Carstairs shook his head. "Not yet. They know of his absence now and it obviously baffles them but no alerts have been sent out. If he doesn't return—"

Thomson said slowly, "It sounds to me as if he's on the run. What would make a man like this—if he *is* our Mr. X—risk everything to live a double life? I only met him last Monday but he struck me as—you'll forgive me, but he struck me as very colorless and frankly dull."

"But organized," put in Carstairs. "Highly organized."

"Money?" suggested Thomson, frowning. "Power?"

Bishop said impulsively, "How about the sheer exhilaration of living a double life?"

"Possible," Thomson said, nodding. "Certainly that would make the money secondary, and if he deals mainly in cables and phone calls, heaven only knows it could be managed long-distance. Tricky but not impossible."

Bishop said flippantly, "It would certainly explain his never marrying if he already has a wife."

But no one was listening. "Since he gives every evidence now of being Mr. X," Thomson said, "I'll alert the office in Chiang Mai. If he's going underground I'd guess that he's heading into the mountains, probably to find Wen Sa, shelter with him and eventually work out an escape route under a new identity. We already know of a Thai general involved in the business, a General Lueng."

Carstairs laughed. "Heard about the coup?"

"No, what coup?"

"Began 6 A.M. Bangkok time, led, we hear, by a General Lueng."

"The plot thickens."

A coup . . . Mrs. Pollifax and Cyrus missing . . . Mornajay in Thailand . . . Listening, Bishop acknowledged that his alarm was mounting, not only at the thought of a traitor in the Department, and Mornajay of all people, but over two people very special to him. He had barely digested the fact that Emily and Cyrus had vanished when it had been followed by Mornajay's mysterious disappearance, and he was still reeling over Holloway's report that the man was seen in Bangkok only thirty-six hours ago. Because Bishop was much fonder of Emily Pollifax than of Lance Mornajay he worried now about a possible connection. He asked himself if Ruamsak's information might have concerned Mornajay's identity as Mr. X, and if this was possible, could Mornajay be behind Ruamsak's murder and the abduction of Cyrus Reed? Once the thought of Mornajay's defection was accepted it brought with it a nightmare of conjecture and worry.

Carstairs said grimly, "I think that in the continued absence of Mornajay we take this conversation Upstairs right now, don't you? I think we have to assume that Mornajay is a very dangerous man now, both to himself and to the Department."

Chapter 10

Dimly Mrs. Pollifax became aware of a man's voice calling out in a strange language, of a woman answering and footsteps running. Tentatively she opened her eyes to see an expanse of red earth, a house with a thatch roof that swept down to nearly meet the ground, a young woman emerging from that house wearing a headdress that dripped silver coins. She closed her eyes; she was not, after all, at home or in bed, and there was something urgent and pressing, something lost that she had to find. Or someone.

When she opened her eyes again she was lying on a mat on the open platform or veranda of a thatch house, and she had not been hallucinating about strange bright headdresses because the woman bending over her was wearing one. Next to the woman stood a man looking down at Mrs. Pollifax, a young man with high smooth cheekbones and intense bright eyes. He was not Bonchoo; he wore wide-legged black trousers and a dark shirt and a knife in his belt, and Bonchoo hadn't looked like this. "Bonchoo," she murmured, and then, struggling to sit up, "Bonchoo?"

The young man called out to someone behind him in the shadows and moved out of sight. Sitting up, Mrs. Pollifax saw that she was virtually surrounded by children and women, all of whom wore the same headdresses and were staring at her in amazement, at her feet, her clothes, her face. Her shoes had been removed and the woman bending over her was applying a cool and soothing paste to the blisters on her feet. Her headdress was so near to her that Mrs. Pollifax's eyes could wander in awe over its intricate rows of hammered-silver circlets, its lines of tiny white buttons and red beads, all fringed by silver coins, the headdress rising to a peak in a cone of marvelous embroidery and a flash of red feathers. Feeling her glance the woman looked up and smiled shyly. Her face was small and worn, but sensitive, with a sweetness that surprised Mrs. Pollifax.

The man's call brought Bonchoo, and seeing Bonchoo again, that broad enigmatic face with its scar and its absurd hat, she felt a flood of relief and affection. "Bonchoo," she repeated, smiling.

He was followed by a gnarled little old woman wearing an identical headdress except that hers was shabbier but no less resplendent. "She brings water," Bonchoo told her, pointing to the jug the woman carried. "She boiled it for you, I saw to that. Treat it like gold, and not too much at once."

The old woman beamed at her, nodding vigorously as Mrs. Pollifax clutched the jug and drank. The water was still warm, and when she had assuaged some of her thirst she put the jug down to cool but she kept a hand around it possessively.

"Next she says you must drink this," Bonchoo told her, holding out a cup hollowed from the burl of a tree. "It's herb tea—altitude-medicine for the heart."

She tasted it, made a face but obediently emptied the cup and to her surprise almost at once her heart stopped fluttering and steadied to a slower, stronger beat. She said in astonishment, "I do feel better, it works, please thank her. Bonchoo, I apologize for fainting but tell me what's happened, have you seen the headman, can we leave now?"

He squatted down beside her. "You have seen him, too, he was here a minute ago, this is his house." He pointed to where the young man had stood. "His name is Nouvak; he's a bright young man who knows how to deal with things."

"Yes but can we leave? Bonchoo, they can't be far ahead of us, Cyrus and the—"

He held up a hand. "Wait—Nouvak will tell you, he knows things. We are in luck, he speaks Thai, Akha, Hmong, some Shan and some English."

"English!" This seemed a miracle indeed in this remote mountain village.

The older woman had retreated, taking the children with her. The younger woman sat back on her heels and spoke words that neither she nor Bonchoo understood. "What is she saying?" Mrs. Pollifax asked. "Can you thank her?"

A voice behind them spoke. "I thank her for you, she is my wife Apha." It was Nouvak, returned, and after he spoke to his wife she gave Mrs. Pollifax a last timid smile and disappeared into the house.

Nouvak sat down beside Bonchoo and regarded her gravely. "I am *buseh*—headman," he said. "My English words not much useful, I practice, okay?"

"Please, yes."

He proceeded carefully, frowning over each word. "Bonchoo say you have lost a *sahmee,* a—"

"Husband," put in Bonchoo.

Nouvak nodded, studying her face. "And you seek for him."

"Yes." Bonchoo had been right, she thought, clearly these were the eyes of a man who "dealt with things," they were alert, intelligent, bright.

"And bandits seek you also, Bonchoo say."

She darted a quick glance at Bonchoo but his face was impassive. "Yes—two men."

"With guns? They have guns?"

"I don't think so," she told him and glanced questioningly at Bonchoo.

Bonchoo said, "If they had guns they would have shot us. No guns."

She did not want to talk about guns. She said, "You've all been very kind but can we go now?"

"Go?" Nouvak looked astonished. "But night comes!"

Bonchoo intervened. "He's right, it's not safe in the jungle at night and you need rest. He has said we may stay the night. Tell her what you've done, Nouvak."

"Yes. Already I send two men to the forest," he said. "To seek for *farang* and two Shan."

"For Cyrus!" she murmured happily.

"Also I have sent four mens to—to—"

"Guard?" suggested Bonchoo.

Nouvak grinned, suddenly boyish. "Okay—yes. Up trees to guard village for bandits. No, *watch* for bandits. My English— too slowly it returns! Now the *dzoema* comes and we talk."

"*Dzoema,*" repeated Mrs. Pollifax doubtfully.

Bonchoo translated. "He tells me that in this village, in all Akha villages, the headman—the *buseh*—is the man who deals with the outside world, with the government people, with the Chinese merchants who come to buy or sell, with the selling of rice and cloth to buy iron to make knives and rifles and machetes and such matters. It is the *dzoema* who guides the life inside of the village and governs it."

"Ah—I see," said Mrs. Pollifax, and feeling better now she moved to sit cross-legged, her feet tucked under her. An excruciatingly thin man was striding across the compound toward them, looking dusty and tired as if he'd been fetched from a faraway field. He gave her and Bonchoo a shrewd glance and sat down next to Nouvak, his eyes on Mrs. Pollifax. He and Nouvak began speaking together, with Bonchoo listening attentively.

They appeared to be speaking about her and she watched the *dzoema* for expressions on his face that might explain the conversation. His skin was dark, the veins on his temple, his neck, his hands and arms standing out in ridges. He gestured frequently in a way that matched his expressive face. Once he laughed and she saw that his teeth were stained red from betal; when he listened he became very still, his eyes searching the face of the speaker.

Bonchoo turned to her at last. "They have been speaking of what is best. They have made us welcome, but hearing of bandits makes them uneasy, they moved here because in their last place they were robbed by bandits of silver, of the money earned from their cash crops, of an M-16 and of two goats."

"Oh dear," she said with a sympathetic glance at Nouvak. "Trouble we don't want to bring them."

"I've told them we can pay well for food, you have money?"

"A lot of 25-*baht* bills," she told him, trying to equate their value in U.S. money.

"Good, five will do for now, they're not rich here as you can see. They have also spoken of this situation. If they find no *farang* and Shan nearby—"

She said quickly, "But if they're not far away they would find them?"

Bonchoo nodded. "Yes but if not, then they offer help in the morning. Probably," he added laconically, "to get us out of here before we bring trouble to them."

"What help?"

"A boy named Anu to guide us. The Akha know the forest and they know the smugglers. He says there is a Shan camp hidden deep in the jungle about twenty li—five or six miles from here, on the Burma border."

She said eagerly, "And they think that's where Cyrus is being taken?"

"Yes but to go there is dangerous," he cautioned. "It's just over the border—another country—and if the smugglers think we spy on them—" His hand chopped the air. "They kill, and who's to know? We die in jungle. We will have to be very bold, and hope."

She looked at him seriously. "For myself I have to go, if Anu will only show me where to go, but you, Bonchoo? Does it frighten you?"

"Frighten!" he exploded. "I have been one scared Bonchoo all day, never *never* will I write letters again or be so greedy—if Wen Sa and my *phi*-spirits let me live."

"And do you think they will?" she asked wistfully.

Bonchoo sighed. "I will hope," he said, and seeing his cheerful face turn somber she thought, *He fights for his future, too: wife, children, work, village, just as I fight for mine: one large, very dear man who likes to read in the bathtub, puts garlic in everything, loves to crouch in the cold to bird-watch—and I love him.*

With a gesture toward Nouvak and the *dzoema* Bonchoo added, "They do this because you lose a husband and your search for him surprises and impresses."

Nouvak's lips curved into a smile. "Our women do not leave the village, it's not Zang. We have proverb: A woman deals with what is between the house and the rice bin, a man deals with what is between other villages and ours."

She wondered what Zang might be.

He rose to his feet. "This is my house, you are welcome," and having said this he walked into the house and disappeared behind a reed partition.

Bonchoo said, "I am going to see if I can buy a machete. Rest, there will be food soon."

But Mrs. Pollifax did not feel like resting, she was curious about this village, and the pain of her blisters had been alleviated by the paste that had been applied to them. Bonchoo and the *dzoema* had strolled to the end of the compound where a young man joined them carrying a machete that Bonchoo began to examine. Stepping into her shoes she winced only a little and walked a few paces to test her strength. Shadows had begun to lengthen in the compound, and the forest behind the village was very still. As she continued walking a dog barked at her half-heartedly and then slunk away. Three girls wearing the ubiquitous headdress and carrying baskets of firewood on their backs came trudging up the path from the forest and stopped when they saw her.

"Hello there," she called.

They looked at each other, giggled and hurried away, darting curious glances over their shoulders. A hen emerged from behind a house, clucking noisily. A naked child wandered into the street, picked up a stick and disappeared among the trees. She felt that she had wandered into a different time warp and this was discon-

certing to her, and yet she felt a sense of great peace that was
healing after a day of shock and tension, as soothing to her jaded
nerves as the herbs that had been applied to her torn foot.

She was peering into a rice bin at the end of the street when
Nouvak walked up behind her. He said almost shyly, "You look
at our village."

"Yes," she said with a smile. "Can you tell me about it?
Bonchoo says you are Akha people, am I rude to ask what that
means?"

He gave her a long look. "Come, I show you a thing," he said.
"And while I show you—you do not recoil?—I practice the English. You walk?"

She nodded and he led her up one of the many paths entering
the village; they ascended to a cleared space and crossed it, coming at last to the path that entered the deeper forest. Here he
stopped and pointed. All that Mrs. Pollifax could see were two
tall tree trunks standing a short distance from the path, scarcely
noticeable against the forest except for a crossbeam that made an
unusual horizontal among so many verticals.

"Our guardian gate," he said. "Very important to Akha, we
have two." Lifting an arm he pointed to the forest. "Outside is
world of danger, inside gates we Akha live happy. The gates
guard us from evil spirits, wild animals, violent death, robbers
and sickness."

She turned to look into his face. "You find so many dangers
out there?"

"It has shown us its dangers," he said simply, "it does not treat
the Akha well." He said this philosophically, without resentment. "We get pushed away, we move many times."

"Doesn't the government here protect you at all? Does it provide schools for you, for instance?"

He smiled briefly. "The school arrives two to three times
monthly but teacher speak no Akha and children speak little
Thai. We are not—what is word?—citizens of this country, we
have to protect ourselves. We do not wish to move down—" He

pointed down the mountain, "we wish to stay free and be Akha, so when people want our land we go."

"And where do you come from?" she asked.

Not understanding, he said, "We come from our first ancestor A-poe-mi-yeh. All our ancestors live with us in spirit, they live with us right now."

Mrs. Pollifax, somewhat jarred by this, glanced around to make sure they were alone.

"We ask for guidance from them," he went on. "We invite them for food and drink at festival times. We live with many spirits, the rice spirit, the harvest spirit, the tree spirit. Maybe we have no written history but we know it—every man must know his ancestors sixty families back in time."

"Sixty generations!" she murmured. "You're not Buddhists, then."

"No—*forest* people!"

"But why, if someone should want your land, do you just go? You have rifles, I have seen them!"

"Because the Akhazang tell us not to fight."

They had begun to stroll back toward the village but at this she stopped. "Akhazang?"

"Yes, we live by its rules. The Akhazang tell us how and when to plant our rice, how and where to build our house, how to hunt the deer and boar, how to live and how to die."

"But—none of this is written?" she said, frowning over this.

"Not written," he agreed, smiling at her. "But still we know. Our ancestors tell us. We learn it from our mother, from our father, from the *pima* and *dzoema*. It is told us many times—we *know*."

She bent down and picked up a pebble. "This too has a spirit?"

"Oh yes! Did you not know?"

She smiled and dropped it into her pocket with the banana skins and eggshells. "Your English keeps growing. Where did you learn it, Nouvak?"

"Mission school, Burma, but when the fighting began—" He shook his head. "That is when I was small boy, now we live here.

The Akhazang say, 'Although a person changes, Akhazang does not change. Although a house is moved ten different places, the ancestor-basket does not change.' " He hesitated and then added, "You are sure they had no guns."

Startled, she said, "Yes."

He nodded. "What we wish is to grow our rice and hunt, make joy with our festivals and raise our children to live by Zang. I am glad you see no guns."

"And what would you do if they came to the village with guns?"

"If we could not make them friendly with our rice wine," he said with a smile, "we would—*woosh,* " he said, pointing to the dense forest behind them. "Always we live with the forest near us to hide in. The trees are our friends, like the sky and the stars and the sun and the rocks."

Touched by his beliefs and trying to remember that for the Akha, too, this was the twentieth century, she gave him the only gift she could think of by saying with great firmness, "They had no guns."

They had reached the compound now. He said, "To sleep in my house—you do not mind?—you must become a grandmother and sleep on the men-side. That too is Akhazang, you are not Akha and must not sleep on the woman-side."

She laughed. "I don't mind, I will be a grandmother in your house." Down at the far end of the compound she saw Bonchoo seated on the platform of Nouvak's house smoking a large cheroot, his feet dangling: this was a new Bonchoo, affable and relaxed, content in the moment.

Whereas I, an American, she thought ruefully, *want instant results, I can be grateful for rest, food and a place to sleep tonight but I cannot shrug off the shadow over my life: I have lost a sahmee.* She called, "Any news yet from the men looking for Cyrus?"

He shook his head. "Not yet, not yet . . ."

Seated on the floor of Nouvak's house they dined on sticky-rice, rolling it into glutinous balls with their fingers and popping it into their mouths. There were small chunks of meat and boiled pumpkin in a bowl swimming with juice but Mrs. Pollifax dared not ask what the meat was, given the poverty of the village and the dearth of animals. Rice wine had been brought out for the occasion and she understood that it was not lightly presented. *"Daw! Daw!"* Nouvak told her cheerfully, which Bonchoo informed her meant *drink, drink.* It had grown dark outside but there was enough light from the hearth to illuminate the house, which amazed her, being made almost entirely of bamboo. The overhead beams were laced with straps of bamboo; baskets hung from a woven bamboo ceiling, they sat on mats of bamboo on a bamboo floor, and the partitions that divided the house into kitchen, men's side and women's side were made of bamboo, all of it cut, woven, spliced and tempered by hand.

Outside, through the slits in the wall, she could see a half-moon rising . . . underneath the house she could hear a pig grunting as he foraged for the scraps of food that fell through the seams. She was aware of a number of children peering in at them over the floor of the veranda, whispering and giggling as they watched the guests: she and Bonchoo were an attraction. It was seven o'clock, the end of a day that had begun so innocently with Cyrus in a luxurious hotel in Chiang Mai, and now she was to sleep in an Akha village deep in the forests of the north. The contrast was palpable. Bonchoo, in the meantime, had begun talking in what he explained in an aside was country Thai, and after the men had laughed uproariously several times she asked to know what he was saying.

"Our Thai folktales are not for women's ears," he explained with a grin. "Very earthy. I am paying for our dinner with my wondrous stories."

Mrs. Pollifax, feeling ungenerous, wondered what she might do to pay for her share of their hospitality; there was only one possibility and as the fire dimmed and the children began to yawn in the rear she told Bonchoo, "I know a few magic tricks."

He looked at her in surprise and a dawning alarm. "But they live very close with spirits here, what do you mean?"

She told him.

"Aha—*gohn lamet!*" he told Nouvak.

"See dahn?"

Bonchoo shook his head. "No, no—*see kow,* white magic."

"What is this?" Nouvak asked her seriously. "You show us?"

Mrs. Pollifax drew out a coin, held it up for her dinner companions to see, and caused the coin to vanish and then to appear all over again: in midair, and then from Nouvak's ear. There was a long and astonished silence and then a child laughed in delight, and then another. Nouvak grinned broadly. At the sound of laughter the women came in from the kitchen and the children swarmed over the platform to see, while shouts from the compound brought a gathering crowd to stand outside and watch.

Gaining confidence Mrs. Pollifax drew out a 25-*baht* bill, rolled it up, palmed it and leaning forward drew it out of a small girl's mouth. Laughter exploded, mingled with giggles and shrieks. Her instructor at home would undoubtedly be shaking his head and saying, "Clumsy, Emily, clumsy!" but in an Akha hill village what she produced was a miracle of magic, and the children grew so eager that Nouvak had to order them back so that the women could see. Drawing near to the end of her repertoire she began to rue her success but her audience did not mind in the least that she repeated her tricks a second, third and then a fourth time. Bonchoo watched, his eyes warm with pleasure in her, and she learned that no matter what language children spoke, their ooh's and their ahh's were the same in every country. She could not have found a more appreciative audience.

A shout from the forest suddenly interrupted them. Startled, Mrs. Pollifax's coins dropped into her lap and she turned to see two young Akha men hurrying up the path and shouting.

Bonchoo and Nouvak at once rose to their feet; the crowd at the edge of the veranda fell back. There were exclamations and excited bursts of speech.

"What is it?" asked Mrs. Pollifax. "What's happening?"

Bonchoo turned to her, smiling. "They have found him!"

"Cyrus?" she gasped. Her fears and tensions fell away from her and she jumped to her feet, straining to see into the darkness beyond the hearth.

"He's coming now," Bonchoo told her.

Behind the Akha men a paler face shone in the dimness and Mrs. Pollifax stepped eagerly forward.

Abruptly she stopped. "But—that isn't Cyrus!" she cried and then, desperately, "That isn't Cyrus, I don't know who this man is but he's just not Cyrus, not Cyrus at *all!*"

The man they had brought to her stopped and glared at her. In a coldly furious voice he said, "I don't give a damn who I'm supposed to be, I demand an explanation for this outrage. I was sound asleep in my sleeping bag when these two—two *savages*—prodded me with their guns and forced me here. The name's Mornajay, Lance Mornajay, and who the hell are *you?*" he demanded.

Chapter 11

"Emily Pollifax," she snapped, disliking him intensely because he was supposed to have been Cyrus and it was unforgivable that he was *not* Cyrus. What was more, he was arrogant, and obviously an American which made his arrogance especially annoying. He exuded authority: a large man in his late forties with a large pale face and a powerful jaw topped by a leonine head of curly gray hair. He was dressed expensively in exquisitely cut camping clothes: suede boots, faded jeans, denim shirt, and they were all immaculate. An expensive camera was suspended from his neck; he carried a sleeping bag in one hand and wore a backpack across his shoulders.

And he was not Cyrus.

He said explosively, "My good woman—"

"*Not* your good woman," she hurled at him, and as more men came to stand next to him, "Is one of those men your guide?"

His sigh was that of a man goaded beyond endurance by fools. "I don't need guides," he told her coldly, "I've trekked in these mountains before, with and without them." He added hastily, "I'm a photojournalist. Is it due to you that I've been waked up and dragged here? What are you doing here?"

Bonchoo, beside her, murmured, "Deliver me from journalists!"

Mrs. Pollifax said curtly, "I've already introduced myself. This is Bonchoo, and the headman next to him is Nouvak, and the men you called savages were being *extremely* kind and looking for my husband, who is lost."

"Lost?" Mornajay's glance raked Bonchoo. "Can't say much for your guide, then." To Bonchoo he said, "Very poor judgment, allowing a client to wander off, isn't it?" Turning back to Mrs. Pollifax he said, "I suppose you're on one of those Jungle Treks they advertise, but I think you ought to be told that your guide has very unwisely taken you much too far off the beaten track and into quite dangerous territory."

Bonchoo and Mrs. Pollifax exchanged glances and said nothing.

"Is this a Meo village?" he asked, looking around him.

"Akha," she said. "As Nouvak can tell you."

"I assume he doesn't speak English?"

Mrs. Pollifax enjoyed replying to this; very sweetly she said, "Actually he speaks it very well."

Mornajay had the grace to look embarrassed. Extending a hand to Nouvak he said gruffly, "Apologies to you then. I can only tell you it was a great shock to be waked out of my sleep by strange men with guns. Damn alarming, too."

He had a point there, conceded Mrs. Pollifax, and decided to forgive his rajah-like attitude, and his reference to savages, but still she could not like him and there was a strong feeling that he was not apologetic at all but only doing what was expedient.

"Now if no one minds—if I can finally *sleep,*" he said curtly, "I will spread my sleeping bag out on the ground here, and get on with my sleep, for I want to get a very early start in the morning."

"Where are you heading?" asked Bonchoo.

He received no answer. Nouvak had called to someone in the shadows and was speaking now to the gnarled little man who had escorted them to the village. To Mornajay he said, "Lipha gives space to you for sleep in his house."

Tightlipped, Mornajay picked up his sleeping bag, nodded coldly to them and strode down the compound with Lipha. His departure brought silence. The charcoal fire was dying, and the night air growing cool. Several of the men turned and left, the children smiled happily at Mrs. Pollifax and one of them came up to her and touched her sleeve to smile shyly into her face. "Goodnight," called Mrs. Pollifax, as they left with their mothers. Apha came up and touched her arm, her eyes huge, shy and warm, and Mrs. Pollifax followed her inside to the women's side of the house, where Apha pointed to a bowl of water in which Mrs. Pollifax washed her face. She then crossed to the men's side, where Nouvak pointed to a bark-hide mat near the door.

Gingerly Mrs. Pollifax lay down and arranged her tired muscles; it was not so hard a floor as she'd expected, being of flexible bamboo. Dismissing a longing to brush her teeth and climb into pajamas she thought instead about their long day, about Cyrus, about Bonchoo, about the two Shan *naklengs* and Mornajay, but mostly she thought about Cyrus. She remembered that after marrying Cyrus there had come moments during the first month when she had acutely missed her old life, the small apartment in the middle of a city, her Garden Club friends and even Miss Hartshorne, whose managerial tendencies had once terrified her, and then one day she'd understood that Cyrus was missing old rituals, too, and they had talked of it, and after that she'd stopped looking back and had entered the present and stayed there happily. Now, lying on her woven straw mat, she could no longer imagine a life without him, and she had to face the fact that he might not be found. Bonchoo had explained his remark to Mornajay about journalists by saying that in the past several years some thirty journalists had been killed by violence in these mountains; people could simply disappear without a trace. Cyrus didn't speak Thai, he had no means of explaining either his innocence or his identity and she could see that English was not frequently spoken here.

She sighed and tried instead to think of Mornajay. She decided that her predominant feeling about Mornajay was embarrassment that he could be so pompous and rude. Like a bandit he had robbed the village of dignity with his comment about savages . . . savages indeed, she sniffed, and wondered what he was doing in these remote mountains. She wondered, too, what another day would bring. The night was filled with noises: a pig grunted, dogs barked, the bamboo walls creaked and from the jungle came the shrilling of cicadas. She hoped that she wasn't going to be too tired to sleep, and turning over she began counting backward from twenty, very slowly; before she reached eight she had drifted into an uneasy, restless sleep.

It was still dark when she jerked awake: the men were dark sleeping shapes around her but on the other side of the partition the women were stirring. Mrs. Pollifax's eyes closed, she slept again and when she awoke the whole village had come to life: women were calling to one another, dogs barking, she could smell the woodsmoke of many fires, and from the kitchen came the murmur of voices. On this side of the partition only Bonchoo remained; he was sitting up and rubbing his eyes.

"Well, Bonchoo," she said.

"*Yai*—we are still here," he said ruefully. "I hoped if I rubbed my eyes it would all go away." He rose and peered around the partition. "Ah—breakfast!"

Once again Mrs. Pollifax arranged herself cross-legged on the floor and ate from the rice bowl, forming rice into balls that she now expertly tucked into her mouth and swallowed; there were also pickled greens and a refreshing tea. They had just finished when Nouvak appeared, ushering in a young boy of thirteen or fourteen. Both carried long thin muskets.

"Anu," Nouvak said, pointing to him. "He goes to show trail, I borrow him to you."

Anu smiled and nodded cheerfully. He too wore the game bag over his shoulder, but jauntily, with a machete tucked into his belt and the long pencil-thin musket over his shoulder. His face

was round and very dark, his eyes lustrous and his black hair
curly.

Strolling outside Mrs. Pollifax blinked at the liveliness of the
compound, at women at work pounding and sifting rice, weaving, bringing in pails of water, all of them in the curious headdresses that Nouvak explained were called *u coe.* The women
glanced up and smiled, as if the memory of the evening lingered
and still occupied them. She had supposed that Mornajay had
long since left—it was already seven o'clock—but there he was,
striding down the compound, looking incredibly immaculate still.

"Not gone yet?" he said amiably. "Where are you heading
today?"

"West," Bonchoo said.

"West!" Mornajay's eyes narrowed. "That's pretty tricky territory. Did you check it out first with the Thai patrol for insurgents?"

Mrs. Pollifax said politely, "I have to remind you that we're
looking for my husband. Did *you* check with the Border Patrol?"

"Of course not, they'd have insisted on an escort, which would
be tedious and—in my case—unnecessary."

She looked at him curiously. "We're searching for a man, what
are you looking for, Mr. Mornajay?"

He hesitated for just an instant. "For a lost monastery."

"A *what?*"

He said firmly, "A lost monastery. I told you I'm a photojournalist. When not on news assignment I'm putting together a book
of photographs of Thailand's temples, *chedis,* shrines, with ac-
companying text on the Khmer influence, the Indian influence, et
cetera. It would be a tremendous feather in my cap to find and
photograph a centuries-old monastery no one else has seen."

Bonchoo said, "What makes you think there is one?"

"Oh my good man," he said chidingly, "how does one learn
anything? Scholarly research . . . a reference in an old manuscript, a chance meeting with a Border Patrol chap who claimed
to have stumbled across it in the jungle. It would probably date
back to the mid-thirteenth century when Burma was dominant,

and when Buddhist monks moved freely back and forth between
Ava in Burma and Chiang Mai in Thailand. That would predate
the Mangrai's reign, no less! I really must find and photograph
it."

Mrs. Pollifax thought it a pity that his personality tended to be
so abrasive because she could admire his enthusiasm. Seeing that
Nouvak hadn't understood, Bonchoo turned to him and described what Mornajay had been talking about; she thought
Bonchoo looked amused but she was startled when the headman
threw back his head and laughed. A small suspicion entered her
mind that both of them knew already of the monastery but she
tucked the thought away for the moment. "It's time we go, isn't
it?" she asked. "Is Anu ready?"

"Anu?" repeated Mornajay. "Who's that?"

"Our guide."

Mornajay looked startled. "I thought *he* was your guide." He
pointed to Bonchoo.

"No," said Mrs. Pollifax gently, "Bonchoo is a friend, not a
guide. Now if you'll excuse us—" She drew Bonchoo aside.
"What do we owe them for their hospitality and for their lending
us Anu, Bonchoo? I'm so grateful I'd give them too much."

He suggested a sum and she pressed the money into his hand,
but still it did not feel enough to her, and while Bonchoo dealt
with paying Nouvak she went off to find Apha. She found her
pouring mash into a trough, surrounded by piglets.

"Apha," she said. The woman looked up, smiling her shy mysterious smile, and Mrs. Pollifax wished with sudden devoutness
that she could ask her what she was thinking and feeling, what
lay behind that sensitive worn face, what it was like for her, an
Akha woman in this remote village living the Akha way. Wanting to give her something personal she groped in her purse and
brought out her pocket mirror, the cluster of large safety pins
that she carried for emergencies and a lipstick.

Apha looked at them and then at Mrs. Pollifax. She reached
out, drew her hand back, looked again into Mrs. Pollifax's face
and then as her fingers curled around the gifts her mouth curved

into a joyous, radiant smile, she murmured excited words and ran into the house. Mrs. Pollifax called after her, "goodbye!" and went back to find Bonchoo.

Mornajay was still in conversation with Bonchoo. Seeing her he said, "Since you're heading west and have a guide I trust you won't mind if I accompany you for a few miles?"

She was not surprised, she had wondered only if he would ask politely or simply announce his intentions. She said amiably, "If it's all right with Bonchoo and Anu. You've given Nouvak the money?" she asked, turning to him.

"It is done."

As they turned to leave Apha ran out of the house holding something that she pushed into Mrs. Pollifax's hand.

"It's a present," Bonchoo said. "She made it herself, she wants you to have it."

Now it was Mrs. Pollifax's turn to smile shyly and to stumble over words that were all the more fervent because she had never seen anything like what was being given to her: it was a necklace made of black seeds and white shells interspersed with pear-shaped brown gourds and bright red feathers, all strung together on a cord. Without regard for any custom or taboo that she might violate she gave Apha a warm hug. "Tell her," she asked of Bonchoo, "that I will always cherish this, it's lovely. And may her spirits of the forest be with her."

Bonchoo translated this for her and then said crisply, "We go!"

Mrs. Pollifax looked back only once at the cluster of dusty huts still wreathed in mountain mist. Smoke rose lazily from the kitchens; the boys and men were leaving to hunt or to work their distant fields, the women would cook and weave and spin and husk rice and carry water and firewood and welcome the men back at dusk. Everyone had a place, and work to do, she thought, with rules to live by and a tribal culture to guard and share. She would not forget: one day, perhaps while tending her geraniums at home she would remember Apha and the simple harmony in which she lived, but remembering home was to wonder with a stab of apprehension if Cyrus would be there with her when she reached it . . .

They passed the guardian gate, crossed a field of stubble and then Anu led them to a narrow trail that entered the forest, and they were returned to that very different universe of the jungle.

Some half a mile farther they came out on the crest of a hill and Bonchoo stopped, pointing. Drawing up beside him Mrs. Pollifax caught her breath at what lay below them: from this vantage point, this small clearing, the hills slanted away and down like a cover of green corduroy tossed over the rounded knobs of earth and graceful hills, dipping, rising, falling until, far below, the forest reached a valley that lay at the base like the bottom of a cup. She saw, miles below them, a thread of road, a cluster of tiny roofs shining in the sun and all around them the uninterrupted sloping walls of green.

Hearing a click behind her she turned and saw Mornajay taking a photograph. He lowered his camera, frowned over it, adjusted something and took another photo. "Marvelous specimen of *Bambus vulgaris,*" he said.

"Where are we now?" she asked, turning to Bonchoo.

"Very high," he said. "Not just high in the mountains but on your map we are now very close to the top corner of my country. Over there is Tanen Range," he added, pointing, "and over there is Burma. Not far."

"You know," she said, looking into his face, "you speak very good English. Do all—uh—smugglers speak it so well?"

He grinned. "Would you believe I study two years at Thammasat University on scholarship when I am a young man? Five children and a wife ago—that long!"

She was surprised, and started to speak, but Anu was waiting and Mornajay had put aside his camera to join them. They continued walking, leaving Mrs. Pollifax to consider just how a student in a Bangkok university might become—five children and a wife later—a smuggler of teak in northern Thailand. This thought occupied her as the trail dropped away from the ridge and they entered deep forest again, the trees closing in on them, the air growing humid. A rattling of palms startled her, followed by a harsh and raucous scream and a flash of brown and yellow among the trees.

"*Nohk koon fawng!*" called Bonchoo cheerfully. "Speaking bird."

"*Genus Acridotheres,* one of your Asiatic starlings," Mornajay announced authoritatively. "You would probably call it a mynah."

"Probably," said Mrs. Pollifax and turned her head to glance at Mornajay curiously.

"We should also see some *Luscinia Golzii,* or at the very least a member of the *pycnonotidae* family called the crested bulbul," he added pleasantly.

"How nice," she murmured and turned back to the trail. The freshness of their morning's start was beginning to diminish as yesterday's overextended muscles resumed their protest. They walked in single file along the narrow trail, Anu in the lead, Bonchoo, then herself, followed by Mornajay. Her quick glance behind her had shown him to be tireless and she began to resent the pressure of his pace behind her. Bonchoo, she thought, at least had the grace to pant occasionally after negotiating a steep hill but Mornajay hiked uphill with ease and she wondered if he would either pant or sweat, and doubted either. He was, she thought crossly, as inviolate as the knife-edge creases on his khaki slacks; he was probably accustomed to lifting weights each morning or to jogging, a thought especially obnoxious to her because after each steep ascent she worried as to how Cyrus was managing them. If he remained ahead . . . *If* . . .

The trail leveled out; they passed massive teak trees, five and six feet in girth and rising beyond her vision into the sky; bamboos with marvelous fronds at the top, like dust mops; clumps of pampas grass, tall, soft and pale as dandelion fluff, and almost always the palms, rustling secretively as if in conversation among themselves. Her antenna went out to absorb it, her eyes beginning to mark its variety and the infinite patterns that yesterday had struck her as monotonous.

Behind her Mornajay had stopped again; she heard the click of his camera as a brilliant-colored parrot flew away. He said with satisfaction, "Genus *Acridotheres,* a zygodactyl, order of *Psittaciformes.*"

This time Mrs. Pollifax felt deeply and peevishly annoyed, and would have replied tartly if Anu had not held up a hand, muttering several words to Bonchoo.

"Border patrol coming," Bonchoo said.

Once again they plunged through the underbrush, crawling under and over vines, Mrs. Pollifax feeling considerable satisfaction at seeing Mornajay crawl on hands and knees in his immaculate clothes. Up among the treetops a mynah bird squawked and flew away, and a subtle hush came over the jungle. She too heard it now, the thud of feet clad in boots filling the corridor of the trail. A line of men came into view, walking quickly in single file, wearing dull green camouflage uniforms and berets, guns slung across shoulders, ammunition belts thickening their waists. *So young,* thought Mrs. Pollifax, looking into their faces, and quickly looked away lest they feel her glance and peer in among the screen of vines and branches. She thought, *Those are police or soldiers, I ought to rush out and stop them, I should be telling them about Cyrus, demanding they find him. I should be—ought to be—Why am I sitting here watching them silently pass?*

She sat.

To anyone looking for Wen Sa's men, she realized, these dozen soldiers passing by were the enemy, a thought that shocked her with its cruelty. She was under hill-country law now, in territory where soldiers patroled in the safety of groups, where the click of Mornajay's camera could just as easily be the click of a safety catch from a concealed gun and where Akha boys and smugglers of teak hid themselves at the approach of the military, just as Wen Sa's men would hide, too—or shoot. Bonchoo had been right in that respect: only those outside of the law had any chance—and a slim one at that—of finding Cyrus in these miles of densely packed mountains.

The men passed; they waited. Anu at last stood up and parted the vines and they returned to the trail.

"We rest soon," Bonchoo said. "We have walked now two hours."

Mornajay's slacks, she noticed, now held smudges of earth at each knee and she decided that this was kinder to think about than what might be happening to Cyrus.

Twenty minutes later they stopped to rest in a grove of bamboo, well off the trail and in a space where a tall tree had fallen, ripping a hole in the dense forest ceiling to bring light down to this small patch of earth. Without a thought to snakes or crawling things Mrs. Pollifax flung herself to the ground to feel the exquisite relief of being no longer on her feet. Bonchoo had been consulting with Anu, who seemed to speak some Thai, but now he came to sit cross-legged on the ground beside her while Mornajay sat on the trunk of the fallen tree. Surrounded by bamboo, Mrs. Pollifax's eyes moved from one tree to another, following the lines of jointed stalks up to the patch of blue sky above. Seeing the direction of her gaze Mornajay said, "Marvelous specimen of *Dendrocalamus giganteous.* Native to Burma but I daresay we're quite close to Burma now. Fascinating!"

This man has no conversation, she thought crossly. Acknowledging that she was tired and about to be as difficult as he was, she said tartly, "Considering that nine tenths of the earth's population call your *Dendrocalamus giganteous* by the name of bamboo, I don't understand why you have to be so pompous about it."

He said stiffly, "I *beg* your pardon!"

"You should," she told him loftily, and was silent, but indignantly silent.

Anu squatted down at the edge of their circle. Except for the occasional fluttering of leaves high above them the forest was silent, the sunlight falling on clumps of moss, decayed leaves and dried branches. A butterfly twinkled among the vines that had sprung up at the edge of this minute clearing.

"I don't remember so many vines yesterday," she announced. "I feel a little as if I'm in a Tarzan movie."

"Tarzan?" asked Bonchoo, puzzled.

She happily explained Tarzan to him.

Bonchoo, brightening, said, "Like our *Pi Tong Luang,* the Ghosts of the Yellow Leaves!"

"Like *what?*"

"Yes, yes," he said, nodding. "They lived here, here in these very forests, like shadows. Invisible peoples! Sometimes woodsmen caught a glimpse, or loggers stealing the teak, there were always stories." With a glance at Mornajay he said dryly, "Like your lost monastery, *mai?* Then some years ago, not long before I am born, at the time of the big war when the Japanese occupy our country, they were found." He shrugged. "I do not know, maybe hunger drove them forward, or many soldiers came to the jungle."

"Ghosts of the Yellow Leaves?" mused Mrs. Pollifax. "What were they like, are they still"—she glanced into the forest—"still here?"

Bonchoo shrugged. "Who knows? They say there were only maybe five hundred of them left when found. Very shy, very frightened. Very small, too, I hear, but with handsome faces. If they lived in this forest for a long long time—like your Tarzan— they may still be here, why not? It is why they were called ghosts."

Mrs. Pollifax said uneasily, "Watching us even now?"

Mornajay said suspiciously, "How do you know so much about the jungle?"

"Oh I know very little, I'm a river man," Bonchoo told him. "Along the rivers the jungle is like a wall, very dark, very dense, very scary, but always interesting to me. Once I talked to a man who studies such things, such matters as the Ghosts of the Yellow Leaves and our cultures, and he showed me that behind the wall—and it takes a machete to get through—there is . . ." He spread out his arms, ". . . all this. And sometimes now in my—er—business—I have to follow jungle trails, and he was right. Only once have I gotten lost, but—well, never mind, that is another tale."

Mrs. Pollifax wondered if she dared to remove her shoes and decided that once removed she might not be able to put them on again. "You said you had been a student in Bangkok at the university, Bonchoo."

"A scholarship student," he said with a smile. "Would you believe from 1973, for three years, we tried real democracy in my country? It was because of what is now called the October Revolution changing matters, so that I—a poor boy from a farm near Chiang Saen—could go all the way to Bangkok to the Thammasat University, where rich people go."

Mornajay gave him a sharp look of surprise.

"How little I know of your country," said Mrs. Pollifax. "What was the October Revolution?"

"It was first time there was rebellion," Bonchoo explained. "It was first time students marched for democracy against the military government—and those students were children of government peoples, too! They had just begun to see how poor the rest of the country was, so they marched and made noises and the government listened, it was *scared*."

"And that's how you became a student, then!"

He nodded. "That is how I went to Bangkok in 1975—it was a miracle, a wonderland, I tell you! But it didn't last," he said sadly. "The military did not want democracy, it meant they lost control and lost their jobs and their power, so they organized, they planned and in 1976 there came the—the—" He stopped and swallowed hard. "What they did, for three years they organized the—what do you call it, the right wing? They formed Village Scouts and they formed together a group of *naklengs*—hoodlums—and called them the Red Gaur—unemployed peoples who hated students. Bad stories were made up for the newspapers; they called the students Communists. Everyone who criticized was called Communist."

"A familiar ploy," said Mrs. Pollifax dryly.

"And then," he said soberly, "we had a sit-down demonstration at Thammasat. Never do I forget the date—October 16, 1976—each year I remember this. A peaceable sit-in, you know? *No!*"

To her surprise she saw tears rise to his eyes.

"What happened?" she asked quietly.

"The police, they attacked our peaceable sit-down," he said, and his hand went to the long scar on his face. "Many of my friends were hurt, and some die." He shook his head, remembering. "The police trapped us, they threw grenades, they shot guns—my friend Charoon died in my arms, all covered with blood."

Not elephants and temple bells and dancing girls, thought Mrs. Pollifax, hearing the anguish in his voice.

"After that," he said simply, "I came home. I love my country but I think the military will always rule us." He sighed. "I think about this very much."

"And what do you think?" she asked gently.

"That we have much blame," he said sadly. "We Thai are a gentle people, we have what you call master-slave history from our past, when we had many many kings. We depend on authority, we want protection. Our village headman gives us protection and we are ready to serve him because in the village he has the money and power. I speak from knowledge because I am a *phu yai ban* in my village—"

"A what?" interrupted Mrs. Pollifax.

He smiled. "What you would call 'big man.' I try to be honest but many such are not. Someone in Bangkok says the farmers should start a cooperative and it is started. The headman is put in charge and many times he keeps all the profits. Who complains? We are not used to complaining as peoples. The headman has grown rich from this cooperative? *Mai pen dai,* then *he* is the man to serve now, *he* has the money, *he* has the power." He sighed heavily. "Maybe one day when my children are grown there will—"

He was interrupted by a sudden hissing sound from Anu, who

squatted at the edge of their circle. Anu held up a hand, his face very still and listening, his eyes combing the forest around them, and then, *"YAI!"* he shouted, springing to his feet. His shout was fierce and shocking.

It was an alarming moment. Bonchoo, startled, sat down on the ground; Mornajay, who had been sitting, sprang to his feet, and Mrs. Pollifax, sitting, instinctively rolled over and joined Bonchoo as something flew out of the tangle of vines, parting the air with an explosive *swish.*

It was an arrow. It found the only person standing—Mornajay —and embedded itself in the empty camera case slung from his neck; the arrow hung there, quivering and vibrating while Mornajay stared down at it in horror.

Chapter 12

"Down!" shouted Bonchoo. "Get *down!"*

"Get this thing out of me!" cried Mornajay. "Damn it, get it out!"

Muttering angrily Bonchoo seized Anu's rifle and plunged into the jungle, leaving Mornajay still upright and staring in horror at the arrow. Mrs. Pollifax jumped up and went to him, appalled by his pallor. For a moment she assumed that he'd turned white from shock until she saw the blood seeping out around the camera case: the arrow's velocity had been so fierce that it had pierced both the back and the front of the leather case and had entered Mornajay's midriff as well. For a moment she felt sick; it could have killed him.

"Sit down," she told him. "Lie down. *Now.*"

He obeyed, his eyes still fixed on the protruding arrow, and it really was dreadful-looking. Its visible length was something like seventeen inches, which implied an arrow much longer, yet even as she stared at it she could note its strange beauty, the fletch fashioned out of thin strips of bamboo folded with exquisite craftsmanship to lengthen and hasten its flight.

"Anu?" she called, but he retreated from her with frightened eyes.

Bonchoo stumbled out of a network of vines. "They've gone."

"But who?"

He held out a fragment of red cotton. "The *naklengs* left this behind."

"So they found us. Mornajay's bleeding," she told him. "The arrow pierced the leather."

"It did that? And meant for me, of course." He leaned over Mornajay and made a face. *"Mai dai*—nasty! Only a crossbow could do this."

"How deeply did it penetrate, can you see, can you guess?"

Mornajay answered through clenched teeth. "Deep enough. Who were they, damn it?"

"Later," Bonchoo told him, bringing out the Shan knife. "First we cut away some of this arrow so we can see the damage." To Mrs. Pollifax he said, "Hold the arrow tight, very tight."

They knelt on either side of Mornajay while Bonchoo carefully cut the arrow, shortening it by some fifteen inches. With Mrs. Pollifax holding the arrow at its point of entry he sliced around the camera case and removed this, too, gave Mrs. Pollifax a long glance, gently pried away her fingers and with one swift and ruthless motion he pulled the arrow out of Mornajay's midriff.

Mornajay screamed.

"Had to come out," Bonchoo told him, and wiped his forehead with his sleeve. "I do not enjoy this situation, Mrs. Emily."

"Why should you?" she commented dryly, and to Mornajay, "How do you feel? The sooner we get away from here—"

"I can still walk!" he snapped.

She looked at him doubtfully. "Could Anu take him back to the Akha village?"

Bonchoo sighed. "It is Anu who is here to guide us to the Shan camp which is well hidden—of course it is well hidden—and without Anu—" He shivered. "I do not care to spend a night in the jungle."

"You mean we have to choose?" she faltered. "Take him with us or go back?" She sat back on her heels and looked at Mornajay, wanting to be kind and yet, "Bonchoo, we *can't* go back, we've come so far, it's taken so long!" *There ought to be antiseptic for his wound,* she thought, *there ought to be a bandage;* she hoped he wasn't in shock and she hoped the wound wasn't going to become infected because it looked ugly, the skin around it alarmingly flushed and red. "We *can't* go back," she said desperately.

Bonchoo spoke to Anu, who nodded and began cutting a stick of bamboo for Mornajay to use as a cane. They helped Mornajay to his feet; he swayed a little but his lips tightened with resolution and Mrs. Pollifax thought that he had the courage of a man who refuses to acknowledge any weakness in himself.

"I'm okay," he said. "I'll be fine. We've got to go on!"

She gave him an encouraging smile but the thought of Cyrus curtailed her deeper sympathies. They could not spare Anu—Bonchoo was right about that—and they simply couldn't turn back now; it was a hellish situation that she could only rationalize by reminding herself that Mornajay had not been invited to join them but had pressed his company on them. They were going to have to exploit his pride in order to keep him moving, which was not a happy thought, but she had no happy thoughts about Cyrus, either, who she had to believe was still alive somewhere ahead of them.

An unhappy case of triage, she thought drearily, and felt suddenly and unutterably tired.

She saw that Bonchoo was watching her. He said simply, "You must not give out now."

So he guessed. *What a good and decent man he is,* she thought, and gave him a grateful smile. "I know," she told him, and glanced at her watch: it was a few minutes past noon, and they had set out at eight that morning. "Is it far now?" she asked.

Bonchoo spoke to Anu. "He says—I think he says—only two hours from here but he doesn't understand distance. By the sun it will be—" He pointed. "Middle afternoon."

"Good," she said, nodding. "I'm glad to know that, it helps."

"Lean on Anu," Bonchoo told Mornajay, and they began

walking again, but slowly, with Anu and Mornajay setting the pace.

They had covered nearly half a mile of trail when Mornajay began to stumble, and after the third time this happened Anu turned and gave Bonchoo a helpless glance. "What is it?" asked Bonchoo and brushed past Mrs. Pollifax to join him.

Mornajay was swaying on his feet, his face flushed, eyes bright. He said in an aggrieved voice, "I refuse to take that as criticism, first of all because it's not so, and second of all—" He stopped. "Second of all," he began again, and seeing Mrs. Pollifax he looked puzzled. "You're not Chin-Ling," he said. "Where's Chin-Ling?"

Mrs. Pollifax reached out, touched his forehead and winced. "He's burning up with fever."

Bonchoo turned to Anu and asked a question, to which Anu responded at some length, with gestures. When he turned back to Mrs. Pollifax he looked deeply troubled. "He says—" Bonchoo hesitated and then blurted out, "He says the arrow may have been poisoned, dipped in *ya pit*—"

"Poison! Oh dear God," she gasped. "Mr. Mornajay—" But Mornajay had dropped to his knees, where he remained for a moment and then slowly sank back to lie sprawled on the forest floor. Kneeling beside him she cried, "Bonchoo, he's *desperately* ill, we've got to find help!" Even as she spoke the words she realized how ridiculous they were, because where on earth could they find help in a jungle so far removed from civilization? Unless —"What about those rangers who passed us?"

Bonchoo shook his head. "Many miles back and an hour ago, Mrs. Emily."

Anu spoke in a level, matter-of-fact voice and Mrs. Pollifax did not need his words translated for her: from the look on his face and the sound of his voice she knew that he had calmly announced that Mornajay would die.

"But we can't—we *can't* just let him die," she protested. She looked down at Mornajay who was twitching and mumbling now, his face contorted, and she knew there was nothing she could do to prevent this. She had not liked him very much but she could not allow him such a sorry ending.

Bonchoo said slowly, "It is possible—"

She glanced up and saw his face thoughtful. "What is it?" she asked, rising to her feet.

"I don't know," he said with a frown, "but it is possible—" He turned to Anu and spoke, the boy listening gravely; they spoke together for several minutes, Anu inserting words, eyes narrowing, until he suddenly smiled, nodding briskly.

"But where is he going?" she asked in alarm as Anu headed into the grove of bamboo and pushed his way through the ground scrub.

"He is going to climb one of the tallest bamboo and see where we are," Bonchoo said. "We must be very near to the Burma border. *Too* near, maybe."

"The Shan camp? Does he think we're near the Shan camp?"

He shook his head. "Still an hour away, and to the south, he says."

She stood beside Mornajay and waited, trying not to think of the hopelessness of their situation. Through the screen of trees she could watch Anu skillfully shinnying up the trunk of a robust bamboo; he climbed quickly, his head disappeared and then his body and at last his feet and he vanished. The forest had turned silent, but not Mornajay who was struggling to sit up.

"No, Mr. Mornajay," she protested, and Bonchoo knelt to help her. "Try to be quiet," she urged as he stared at her blankly, the pupils of his eyes hugely dilated. "Bonchoo, what is Anu looking for? What did you say might be possible?" As Mornajay sank back with a groan she said despairingly, "He ought to be given an emetic. If it truly is poison—"

"If it's what Anu calls the 'madness poison' it may act slowly," Bonchoo said. "One must hope—" He stopped as a voice called from the distance.

Mrs. Pollifax leaped to her feet. "What was that?"

"It's Anu," said Bonchoo, and shouted back to him.

Anu's bare feet came into view, then his body, then his head as he descended the bamboo, and despite her agitation Mrs. Pollifax marveled at his grace. He jumped the last few feet to the ground and came to them smiling.

"What has he seen?" she asked anxiously.

Bonchoo didn't reply, he was busy hurling questions at Anu. She wished that she spoke Thai, she wished she spoke the Akha language, she wished—"What *is* it, Bonchoo?" she repeated, because Anu's smile had faded, he was shaking his head.

Bonchoo turned to her at last. "There is something I hoped for, maybe half a mile from here, not far. But Anu refuses to go and see, so I must. I will not be long."

She said fiercely, "Go? Bonchoo you're not telling me what Anu saw! Go where?"

He said, "No, because first—please, I must first learn if it is the place I hope it is, a place I stumbled across once, a long time ago, when I was lost. There may be people—trust me," he said, and lifting the machete out of his belt he brushed aside the vines and walked in among the columns of bamboo, except that unlike Anu he continued walking until she could no longer see him.

She stood for a long time staring at the place where he'd vanished, feeling bereft and very alone. She could trust him, couldn't she, he would return, wouldn't he? She glanced at Anu who was watching her, gave him a weak smile and went back to Mornajay.

When she looked again for Anu he was gone.

"Anu?" she called, and then, *"Anu?"*

There was only silence; Anu, too, had vanished, but like a wraith, without a sound. She walked around the fallen tree and peered into the forest; she left Mornajay and walked back to the trail, her footsteps terrifyingly loud to her as she clumsily tripped over branches. She found the trail but it was empty, and returned to the fallen tree and to Mornajay, who was no longer mumbling but obsessively turning his head from left to right as if to free it from an intolerable burden.

She sat down beside him, stunned by Anu's defection and frightened by the thought that he might not return. She thought,

If he doesn't return how can we ever find Cyrus, how can we reach the Shan camp?

"Anu?" she called again.

She wondered if Anu believed that Mornajay had been taken over by evil spirits, or—more optimistically—if he had decided to go with Bonchoo, after all, and was following him.

Or perhaps, she thought with a chill, Anu feared the return of the *naklengs* who had tried to kill Bonchoo and might try again. At this thought she decided that she would not call out Anu's name again but would sit very quietly.

The silence was unnerving; it was as if the forest's animals and insects were asleep while they waited for night, like the snakes Bonchoo had spoken of, but the night was a thought that she found important to avoid. What she had to face and accept was that Anu had slipped away into the forest, and Bonchoo had left without any satisfying explanation, filled with a hope that she couldn't share because what help could he find here, she wondered, and—more important—would she be able to find Bonchoo if he didn't return, would he have cut a path with his machete that she could find?

To occupy herself she began carefully examining her surroundings, listing what her glance absorbed. "That," she said aloud in a low voice, "is a grove of bamboo, and there is a butterfly— lovely—such a tender pale cream color with wings tipped in brown. And along the fallen tree trunk there is a procession of ants going in and out of the hollow in the stump . . . the earth is red where there are bare patches, and there's some sort of ground cover over there and somewhere high above there must be the sky."

Abruptly Mornajay screamed, pointing a trembling hand at something she couldn't see, and it felt to her as if the jungle moved a little, shifted, as if his hallucinating disturbed its unseen occupants as acutely as it disturbed her.

Or had he truly seen something? She remembered the Ghosts of The Yellow Leaves and shivered; were they being watched by men of the forest who knew how to be invisible?

Mornajay's scream made them known just when they needed protective coloring, and her uneasiness mounted. She whispered, "I will count backward from ten to one . . . Mr. Mornajay, I'm going to count backward, try to hear me and please don't shout again . . . Ten . . . nine . . . eight."

A sound of rustling stirred the canopy of leaves overhead, she glanced up furtively and then around her and concentrated again on counting numbers, this time beginning at one hundred and working down, her glance often wandering to the watch on her wrist to count the minutes as they passed, each one assuming the shape of an eternity. Two o'clock arrived. She could feel Mornajay's body heat from where she sat, his whole body radiated heat and she wondered how long a human being could survive such a temperature, and where he had gone in the privacy of his delirium.

Aspirin, we ought to have aspirin, she thought. She had none with her, it was one of many items left behind in the hotel, but since it was possible that Mornajay carried some with him she crept over to his backpack to look. When she turned it over to open she found it surprisingly heavy. Unzipping it she peered inside and then in astonishment she opened it wider: she was looking at a shortwave radio, which explained the weight of it, and at a smaller object wrapped in silk whose shape told her that it was a gun. She lifted out the gun and unwrapped it: it was a 41 magnum revolver. She stared at it for a long time: no pajamas, no aspirin but a radio and a quite lethal-looking automatic . . . this to find a lost monastery? She sat back on her heels, wondering what a man looking for a monastery would want with a radio. The revolver she could understand, considering that he'd come without a guide, claiming an experience in these mountains that implied he knew its dangers, but a radio suggested more than a safeguard against becoming lost. For one thing it was heavy; a compass and a map would be more sensible and she was finding neither. The radio implied a rendezvous, messages, other people and brought the nagging suspicion that Mornajay had lied to them about his purpose here.

It was certainly puzzling but she realized that her speculations were purely academic now because whoever Mornajay was, and whatever had brought him to these mountains, it looked very doubtful now that he would ever leave them. For this she pitied him, and with a sigh she carefully returned the radio and the revolver to his backpack. Returning to her place beside him she began doggedly resuming her counting backward from one hundred back to one.

"Which is extremely tiresome," she complained, having accomplished this, and went on to perform the feat again. She had reached twenty when she heard the distant sound of a machete hacking away at branches, and then came the miracle of a voice. It was Bonchoo, calling to her.

"Bonchoo!" she cried, leaping to her feet. "Oh Bonchoo— *Bonchoo!*"

He was returning . . . With tears in her eyes she watched his broad and bulky shape appear through the screen of trees and vines. He called out, "I have brought help!"

"Help?" she echoed, not understanding, and then to her astonishment she caught a glimpse of orange in the forest behind Bonchoo, and then, another, and two verticals of orange turned into a pair of young men wearing orange—no, saffron, she amended—saffron robes. *"Monks?"* she gasped. She wanted to cry, she wanted to laugh, but with a semblance of calm she went to meet Bonchoo, and as he emerged from the tangles she grasped his hand. "I'm so glad to see you," she said, and promptly burst into tears.

Bonchoo, embarrassed, patted her shoulder. "How is Mornajay?"

"Worse," she sobbed and drew out a handkerchief and blew her nose. The two young monks walked into the clearing carrying a bamboo stretcher. They looked very young, still in their teens, their heads shaved, smiles very white in their dark faces. "Where on earth did you find them?" she asked.

"Later," he said. "We must hurry while there is still hope."

The monks put down the stretcher next to Mornajay, placed

fingertips together in a *wai* and bowed to her, then gently lifted
Mornajay onto the stretcher.

"Where is Anu?" asked Bonchoo, looking around in surprise.

"Gone. He didn't catch up with you? He just *went.*" She
picked up Mornajay's camera and his sleeping bag and waited
while Bonchoo absently picked up Mornajay's backpack.

"Not good," he said with a sigh. "He must have been scared
the *naklengs* would come back and kill us all. Scared for himself,
because if an Akha dies outside his village—" He shook his head.
"They fear this most of all."

She said sadly, "Not finding the Shan camp frightens me most
of all. Bonchoo, where are we taking Mornajay, where on earth
do these monks come from?"

"You will see," Bonchoo said, brightening. "To find the temple
—I scarcely dared hope, but the spirits of the forest are *go rooh
nak* after all. It's a miracle. Six years ago when I was smuggling
radios into Burma and was lost I stumbled across the ruins of
this *wat . . .* we are very near to the border now."

"A ruined temple, and *inhabited?*" she said in awe.

"Only by the Acharya, a very holy man, and the few who
come to learn from him, like these two." He added as they passed
with Mornajay, *"He* might call it the lost monastery he seeks,
who knows? Now I will go first, with the machete."

He went to work at once, widening the path for the stretcher,
and they set out with Mrs. Pollifax following behind the two
monks. A weight had been lifted, and she experienced an infinite
relief that something could be done for Mornajay after all, and
that if he must die it would be with a few amenities, and with a
holy man present. They walked quickly; Bonchoo had cut a good
path on his first journey and it was only occasionally that they
had to stop for him to cut away more undergrowth. The gloom of
the jungle was deepening, however, and Mrs. Pollifax shivered at
the thought of darkness arriving before they found shelter. Overhead a faint breeze stirred the foliage; birds flew away at their
approach; in this dim light she thought it was rather like moving
through an aquarium that had lost the overhead rays of sun.

They went so swiftly that it was a surprise to her when they suddenly walked out of the jungle's gloom into the golden sunlight of late afternoon.

She stopped in astonishment. Ahead of her three seated Buddha-images rose out of the ground, massive in size and towering over the vegetation that already engulfed their base; three stone Buddhas seated in a row, at least twenty feet high, serene and dreamlike in their tranquility, each with lips curved in a tender smile, and here of all places, in the middle of a jungle. She gazed up at them in amazement, at their colors faded and weathered into dull shades of ocher and rust, at faces marred by erosion but still clear, and she wondered for how many centuries they had sat here in dreamlike contemplation, how many sunrises and sunsets they had watched come and go and how many civilizations as well. "How astonishing, how beautiful," she whispered.

The two young monks were just disappearing beyond the Buddhas but Bonchoo had stopped; he had slid to his knees, his hat removed, and he was bowing three times to the Buddhas, his face intent and reverent. This was a Bonchoo she'd not seen before and she waited, not wanting to encroach. When he rose to his feet he bowed a last time and she followed him past the huge stone images, feeling very small beneath them and still marveling at their being here. The path led into a tired-looking garden and seeing the temple beyond it she stopped again and stared.

Once it must have occupied many acres of ground but only a third of the building remained standing, and much of this in ruins. Its outer skin had been stripped away by time and erosion, leaving thick slabs of laterite that glowed brick-red in the sun, many of the stones hurled to the earth as if a giant fist had scattered them. With so much of the *wat* crumbled into dust and slab almost all of the roofs had vanished, but where the walls remained standing the roofs had been replaced by intricate arrangements of bamboo and thatch, giving the impression of large untidy birds' nests dropped from the sky. From the walls that had survived, however, she could discern the shape of what had once existed here: two stone griffins still guarded a staircase that led up to a wide parapet, and beyond this rose the spire of a *chedi,* which must have been what Anu had seen when he climbed the bamboo half a mile away. Off to her left above the trees a brilliant orange sun was slowly sinking into the jungle.

Three stone Buddhas dreaming in a row . . . the ruins of an ancient temple . . . an orange sun . . . She was caught by the surprise of it, and by a feeling of enchantment that swept over her, as if she had stumbled into a space where time no longer existed. The isolation, her sense of discovery, the unexpected and powerful beauty of it held her spellbound. For a moment she, too, was released from time as she stood among the ghosts of the centuries, and with this there stole over her a sense of wonder that life had led her to this holy place, this temple guarding a past that was all but forgotten by the world. A movement on the parapet caught her eye and she glanced up to see a man observing her. He was, she thought, the one detail that had been missing from the scene and which completed it, a man in a saffron robe, his head shaved; perhaps it was the holy man, she thought, but she was not close enough to see more, and once seen he vanished. With this she emerged from her trance and remembered why she was here.

She was alone. Bonchoo had disappeared and so had the two monks carrying Mornajay. She chose an arched entrance under the staircase and entered a long dark corridor. Following a sound of low voices she mounted narrow stone stairs that brought her to a room that was roofed with thatch and opened onto the parapet. The late sunshine filtered through the slats of bamboo in thin gold stripes. Mornajay lay restlessly on a mat, surrounded by Bonchoo and the two young monks. The man she had seen on the parapet had his back to her as he leaned over Mornajay examining him. She could not see his face but she could see that he was holding one of Mornajay's hands and gently squeezing the fingernails. He nodded and spoke to his two monks, who handed him a bowl and a cup.

Bonchoo, seeing her, rose and took her by the arm. "Come," he said, "it's better you not watch. While I went back for you there was time for the Acharya to make antidotes. Trust him, he is a very holy man."

"But what can he give Mornajay *here?*"

Bonchoo chuckled. "Just now it is *nguang chum, hua euang* and *krachao sida* boiled in water, does that help?"

"No," she said with a wan smile.

"Me either but this is what I am told. What *nguang chum* is I don't know—some sort of herb only country people know—but *hua euang* and *krachao sida* are kinds of orchids."

"But does he think Mornajay will live? I mean, it's surely been two hours at least!"

Bonchoo said gravely, "It will be decided by his karma but because it has been two hours and because he did not die the Acharya says it must have been weak poison."

"Weak! I shudder at the thought of a powerful dose! Does the holy man speak English?"

"A little, I think."

"Only a little—oh dear," she sighed.

They walked out onto the parapet into the soft cooling air. Here they were at eye level with the tops of the trees surrounding the clearing. The orange globe of sun had slipped into the forest, leaving the sky suffused with pink. A flock of rooks flew down and encircled a huge tree at the edge of the forest, swooping and diving and twittering until they settled in among its leaves. A parrot protested their invasion and flew away with a flash of scarlet and green. As they stood and watched, the pink sky faded into a luminous mauve. Except for the birds and a few chickens scratching in the garden below there was only the hush of twilight.

She dared at last to ask the question that concerned her. "We've lost Anu, Bonchoo. Are we near the Shan camp, could one of the young monks take us there in the morning, would they know where it is?"

Bonchoo hesitated and then he said carefully, "They are giving us a corner to sleep in tonight, and there will be food. We are interruptions," he told her, turning to look into her face. "We have brought the world here, *Koon* Emily. Of course the Acharya must know the Shan camp, but whether he will concern himself with such worldly matters I don't know. He is a very holy man. I think we must wait to present this problem to him in the morning, Mrs. Emily."

A second night, and tomorrow a third day . . . she stared unseeingly now into the jungle and thought how every hour made finding Cyrus more problematic. Yet Bonchoo was right, she conceded this; there was nothing that could be done now with night coming, nothing at all.

But holy man or not, she thought grimly, the Acharya *must* be persuaded to help them in the morning.

Chapter 13

Sometime in the night Mrs. Pollifax grew restless and awoke to find that the jungle had awakened, too; a surging cacophony of cicadas rose from the forest, providing the backdrop for a confusion of other sounds: the fierce cry of a bird, a sudden, nearly human scream followed by a number of howls and then a drop in decibels to the steady drone of cicadas before the quarrels and conversations began again. Her gaze moved across walls striped with moonlight filtering through the roof of woven bamboo slats, and she thought automatically, *They'll have to repair that before the rainy season.*

Mornajay had quieted several hours ago. Turning her head she could see his dark form lying only a few feet away from her, and Bonchoo curled up on his mat by the door—Bonchoo who had told her without the least chagrin that he would not be happy to sleep in a cubicle of his own because he might wake up in the night to find a ghost occupying the mat with him.

She had been very tired when she lay down and she was not sure whether it was the night sounds of the jungle that had waked her, the dull ache in her legs from yesterday's long walk, or the smallness of their evening meal, which had consisted of broth with a few noodles and scraps of chicken in it, and a bowl

of rice. She had not seen the Acharya again. There appeared to
be five novices on the premises, two of whom had prepared and
brought them their dinner and had then withdrawn.

She thought, *There's no point in lying here and puzzling out
why I'm awake . . . I'm awake.*

She crept over to Mornajay and placed a hand on his forehead,
hoping his temperature might have fallen a notch or two, and for
one awful moment believed he was dead; his flesh was cool.
When she grasped his pulse and found it beating steadily she sat
back on her heels and stared down at him in amazement: his
fever had broken, there were still miracles abroad, the Acharya's
herbs had proved strong medicine or perhaps, as Bonchoo had
said, it was not in Mornajay's karma to die today.

A loud snore from him abruptly changed her mood of awe; she
smiled and left him to his sleep, found her shoes and tiptoed past
Bonchoo out into the dark stone corridor. Emerging on the parapet she met the beauty of a perfect full moon, a brilliant globe of
light suspended like a lamp over mountains and jungle, outlining
both in silhouette-form, like paper cutouts black against the night
sky. The luminous light threw a silvery path across the parapet,
made all the more brilliant by the black shadows of the monastery walls. It tipped the broken spire of the *chedi* with a ghostly
silver light and turned the pockmarked gardens below into a
bright moonscape. A bird called out from the jungle; the air was
soft and cool on her face, and there were stars in the west so low
and bright she felt she need only reach out to grasp one. She
stood among the harlequin patterns of black and silver and
looked for a long time at the sky.

With a glance at her watch—it was one o'clock in the morning
—she strolled to the left, rounded a corner and came to a stop,
discovering that she was not alone. The Acharya was seated on
the parapet at a point where the low wall had crumbled away; he
sat calmly erect, his legs crossed under him in the full lotus
position, hands folded in his lap as he gazed out at the jungle, the
sky, the moon. He sat without movement, rooted there like one
of the Buddha-images beyond the garden, his orange robe dark-

ened by shadows but his profile clearly illuminated by the moonlight. It was a profile not unlike those etched on a Roman coin, lean, powerful, ascetic.

Without knowing why, without being able to explain her action, Mrs. Pollifax moved softly toward him until, some ten paces behind and to one side of him she too sat down, crossed her legs under her and closed her eyes . . . and almost at once, seated there, she became aware—and knew—that she truly did sit in the presence of a holy man because she had never before felt so at peace, or felt such love and serenity flowing into her from him. Time stood still again as she moved without thought through depths she'd never experienced before.

It ended only when her left foot protested against the weight of her right leg, for the lotus position was still unmanageable for her. The pain of it returned her to the moment, and opening her eyes she looked again at the Acharya's profile silhouetted against the trees beyond the parapet: he sat undisturbed. Glancing at her watch she saw that an hour had passed, she had sat for that long a time. Silently she rose and left, and returning to her mat on the floor she lay down and slept deeply and restfully, utterly relaxed and without worry, until the sun reached her face.

Opening her eyes she saw Bonchoo leaning over Mornajay.

"*Koon* Emily—Mrs. Emily," he said in a whisper, "he sleeps, the fever has gone."

"Yes," she said drowsily, and sat up and rubbed her eyes. "Can you speak to the holy man now about finding the Shan camp, Bonchoo? We could get started soon, we must be very near it."

Bonchoo nodded. "I could, yes, I am more hopeful. He has had the *namjai* to feed and shelter us, he may have the *namjai* to help us."

"What does *namjai* mean?"

He grinned. "To turn into English would be 'water of the heart.'" He rolled up his mat, placed it in a corner and vanished down the corridor.

Oh for a toothbrush, lamented Mrs. Pollifax. She reached into her purse for a comb and was about to begin her morning ablu-

tions when she saw that Mornajay's eyes were open. "Good
morning," she said, and went to him.

Mornajay stared at her, ran a tongue over his lips and tried to
speak. His voice was a whisper. "Thank you."

She nodded. "You're a very lucky man, Mr. Mornajay, but I'm
not the one to thank."

His eyes moved to the thatched roof and he frowned. "Where
am I? What has happened?"

"Well, I think you've found your lost monastery," she told him
with a smile.

"My what?"

"Your lost monastery. You said you were looking for a lost
monastery."

"I was?" He looked puzzled. "How did I get here?"

"Better you sleep," she told him, patting his arm. "Just sleep
and get well, there's time later to—"

"Time!" His eyes opened wide and he struggled to sit up,
stirred by some inexplicable urgency. "What day? What date is
this? Please—important!"

"Let me think a minute," she said. "Yes, this would have to be
Saturday morning, which makes it the nineteenth of January."

"Good—all right, then. Yes—sleep. Get strong." He smiled
faintly. "Never so weak before. Dysentery? Malaria? Typhoid?"

She laughed. "I don't think you'd believe me if I told you, Mr.
Mornajay. Just sleep and be glad."

"Glad," he murmured and closed his eyes. "Yes, glad," he
repeated and fell asleep.

She came closest to liking him at this moment. He was not an
easy man to like, she thought: stiff, cold, estranged, concealing
every hint of the vulnerability that she was seeing now. She
thought he would be a happier and better person if he acknowledged his humanness instead of keeping it sealed up inside of
him. On the other hand, she thought, one could never know the
traumas that shaped such people; everyone carried around with
them their own particular defenses, antagonisms, secrets and un-
certainties, and if Mornajay seemed to carry an unusually heavy

load of them he at least, she thought with humor, wore beautiful clothes, and very expensive ones.

She left Mornajay to search for food. They had slept late, it was nearly nine o'clock, and she supposed that in a temple or monastery this was very late indeed; the Acharya had no doubt been up since dawn, or perhaps had not slept at all. She found the kitchen, or what she assumed to be the kitchen because the room held a circle of bricks on the stone floor, with the embers of a fire still glowing, and a large lacquered bowl with rice soaking in it. Two kettles hung neatly from a peg on the wall; there was a shelf with eight carved wooden bowls on it, and eight empty mason jars. In a corner stood a small pile of kindling for the fire, and above it a finger of bananas hanging from a nail. She removed one and hungrily ate it standing there.

Finding no one at all, not even Bonchoo, she returned to the parapet and descended the lion-guarded staircase to the garden, following a path that led to a stand of trees in the rear. A well stood here in the shade, efficiently made of cement, with a primitive pump and an intricate series of bamboo pipes to carry water into the nether regions of the monastery. A cluster of unused bamboo pipes lay about like jackstraws, and seeing the ditches that threaded the bare garden she realized that in the planting season those pipes would be attached to the well and would feed water to the garden, irrigating the rice and vegetables.

As she neared the well she saw Bonchoo sitting on its step, looking gloomy.

"Bonchoo!" she called.

He made room for her and she sat down beside him. "Did you find the Acharya?"

He pointed to three saffron robes hanging from the branch of a tree. "Yes, he was doing his laundry. Now he has gone to teach boys in one of the rooms."

"And?"

He turned to her with a melancholy sigh. "He will meditate on it; he says he cannot encourage anger against the Shans, he does not—without meditating on it, you understand—feel he can show us where they may be."

"And when is he going to meditate on it?" she demanded. "You said he'd gone off to *teach?*"

Bonchoo nodded.

"This shocks me," she said quietly. "I don't understand it when he was kind enough to help Mornajay."

Bonchoo lifted his hat, rubbed his head, sighed and placed his hat more squarely on his head. "He says he lives here in peace and harmony with the mountain people. He teaches reading to the young men who come here, he serves the Thai people who find their way here, he feeds the bandits and gives shelter to the insurgents, and benediction to smugglers as well as to soldiers who pass by. He does not judge because every man has the Buddha nature."

She said hotly, "That's all very well, but did you explain that those neighbors of his with the Buddha nature have kidnapped my husband and may very well kill him, and that two of them have tried to kill you?"

He turned and looked at her. He said gravely, "It is most difficult. We bring him a man poisoned by an arrow, we ask help, he knows nothing of us except that we bring violence with us. We must wait. He is a holy man, *Koon* Emily. He will meditate on it; if it is his karma to help, he will help."

"How will he know?" she said bitterly.

"He will know." Frowning over this Bonchoo said earnestly, "Even I can see—if he takes us to a secret camp something changes here. He must be a man trusted with many secrets. I can be sad, but do not despair, Mrs. Emily. If the Acharya refuses us we can still set out alone, the two of us. Anu said south—"

"Could one of the young monks be persuaded to guide us?"

"Only if he asked them to," Bonchoo said sorrowfully.

"And would it be dangerous, just the two of us?"

He said dryly, "Only if we cannot find the trail, or the way back if we become lost."

She nodded and rose. "I will speak to the holy man myself. You said he spoke some English?"

"Quite much, really."

"Oh? Where can I find him?"

Bonchoo gestured toward the building. "He went in."

She found the classroom, a long room, very dim and bare, the only points of light the brilliant sunshine framed in the squares of two windows, whose shutters had been thrown back for the light, and the brightness of the five orange robes worn by the novices. Four of them lay on the floor turning the pages of a manuscript; the fifth sat cross-legged beside them, reciting in a sing-song voice. He glanced up at Mrs. Pollifax and smiled. She returned his smile but left because the Acharya was not among them.

She found him at last in the kitchen, ladling out the rice that she had seen soaking on her earlier visit. He was ladling it with a spoon into a steamer made of woven bamboo. Hearing her he turned, and for the first time she was seeing him face to face. She thought how conditioned one became to seeing hair on a person's head, and yet a shaved head certainly placed emphasis on the face, and what a striking face his was. He did not look at all Asian: French, perhaps, she thought, or—not familiar with the Burmese—he was perhaps a Burman. If he was a Thai then his blood had been well mixed with Caucasian for many generations. It was a very strong face—strong, *strong,* she repeated—the skin brown but whether from birth or the sun it was hard to guess. The eyes were brown, too, soft and penetrating. She wondered if he had been aware of her presence during the night when she had sat behind him in the moonlight. "Do you speak English?" she asked.

"Not lately," he said in a pleasant voice without accent, "but yes I know English."

And speaks it very well, she thought in surprise. Speaking slowly she said, "My name is Emily Pollifax and I'm a tourist from the United States visiting your country. I came with my husband, and now I've lost him."

He nodded attentively.

"He was placed in a car—against his will—in Chiang Mai," she told him, watching his face to be sure that he understood. "And Bonchoo and I followed this car."

He nodded.

"Twice," she went on, indignation creeping into her voice, "twice men have tried to kill us. Once on the road and once here in the jungle. It's these men who have abducted my husband, or friends of theirs. We've been told that the Shan could be taking him to a camp nearby. We beg your help. To find the camp, to find my husband."

He said gently, "Food and shelter and healing I give freely to anyone who comes here. But to direct you to the Shan camp would betray the people I live among, it would betray their trust, especially if you wish them harm."

"I wish them no harm," she told him, beginning to feel desperate. "What harm could Bonchoo and I bring them? I just want my husband!"

He looked puzzled. "But what do they want of Mr. Pollifax?"

"Not Pollifax," she said impatiently, "his name is Reed—Cyrus Reed—and as to what they want—" She stopped in midsentence because she saw that she had startled him.

"Cyrus Reed?" he repeated. "You say you are American?"

"Yes, from Connecticut, and for myself I say again that I wish no harm to the Shans, I just want Cyrus *back."* She would have said more but he held up his hand for silence, turned away from her and picked up the wooden ladle again. She stood and watched impatiently as he spooned wet rice into the steamer; her impatience began turning into anger as he added more kindling to the wood set under the wok, relighted the fire and added a pinch of salt to the rice.

When he turned back to her his face was impassive. He said in a strange, nearly sing-song voice, "I will have Prasert show you where the camp is but . . . when the sun is higher, after we have eaten rice."

She could scarcely believe it. She realized that she'd been holding her breath and now she expelled it in a long sigh of relief. She could have hugged him, she would at least have liked to shake his hand but he stood stiffly, very formal now, his face shuttered. She said with feeling, "Thank you, thank you *very* much."

He nodded and turned back to his work.

To Bonchoo she said triumphantly, her heart singing, "We leave after we've eaten rice."

Happily now she wandered, the monastery suddenly a different place, an experience that she must tell Cyrus about—she did not allow herself to think he might not be found today—and so she roamed freely from room to room, walking around the ruins, examining the irrigation system in the garden, entering the building again by a small arched doorway she'd not seen before, and finding a room that she'd not seen before.

It was a small room, and very plain: a mat for sleeping, a low table with a candle, a shelf, the roof a screen of woven bamboo through which the sun sent spangles and sequins of light. One of these spangles of light fell on a second shelf on which stood a few books and Mrs. Pollifax, deciding that this must be the Acharya's room, moved toward the books, curious as to what a holy man would read in this isolated corner of the world.

There were six books, three of them very old, their pages tied together between boards, and from the exotic loops of print she guessed they were manuscripts written in Thai, or Pali, the language of Buddhism. The fourth book's title was in French— French, she murmured, startled—and then turning to the last two books she was delighted to find that both were in English, a worn paperback of Shakespeare's *Tragedies,* the other a dog-eared hardcover copy of Rudyard Kipling's *Kim.* Her hand went out to the last two and then drew back: *I shouldn't be here,* she thought, *I shouldn't have entered this room and invaded the Acharya's privacy.*

On the other hand, she thought, *I did, and I'm here,* and because she loved the book *Kim,* too, and because the copy looked the most used, most read and most loved of them all, she reached out for it and took it down from the shelf.

It was a child's edition of the book, with illustrations by a long-ago artist familiar to her from her own childhood; she had never seen an illustrated copy before and she turned the pages, smiling, until she reached the frontispiece on which an inscription had been printed.

In a child's block letters she read:

MY BOOK.

FROM MAMA ON MY BIRTDAY.

JOHN LLOYD MATTHEWS.

Chapter 14

Down the dark stone corridor she fled, returning the way she had come, and breaking into a run when she saw the arched doorway ahead. Outside in the bright sun she sat down in the shade of the well and caught her breath. She told herself that the inscription in the book was meaningless, that John Lloyd Matthews had spent years—decades—in Thailand before he disappeared, and that once he'd been declared legally dead it was only natural that some of his possessions had remained in the country to make their way into the marketplace and be sold to strangers.

A man like the Acharya would certainly appreciate a used copy of *Kim,* found in a bookstall or bazaar. The book had not had to travel far, after all, because John Lloyd Matthews had disappeared in Chiang Mai.

He had been Cyrus' friend, she remembered, and he had been abducted too, or so they believed, and she could certainly see now how easily it could be done.

She thought, *Perhaps Matthews was reading the book when he was abducted, and his murderers brought it into the mountains and someone left it with the Acharya. Or perhaps . . .*

Still shaken by the inscription she thought, *Stop—Stop and look at this sensibly!*

But it was impossible to sort out the astonished thoughts bombarding her: the Acharya did not look Thai, or Chinese, or even Asian, and he spoke excellent English. The holy man had told Bonchoo that he could not help them because he lived in peace with his neighbors. When she had accosted him herself he had repeated this, telling her very flatly that he couldn't help them, and then . . . NOT *Mr. Pollifax,* she had flung at him, *his name is Cyrus Reed.*

And abruptly everything had changed, he had looked startled and turned away, and when he turned back he had agreed to let one of the monks guide them to the Shan camp.

Cyrus had said, *We grew up together, same high school in Connecticut, we called him Joker Matthews.*

Cyrus Reed, the Acharya had repeated, and then, *You are American?*

Bishop had said, *There was never any clue to what happened, the theory now is that he was abducted for ransom, struggled and was killed and buried in the jungle.*

My book. From mama on my birtday. John Lloyd Matthews.

Impossible, she thought.

She emerged from her convoluted thoughts to realize that Bonchoo was calling to her from the parapet. She called back, "Yes?"

"I have given *Nai* Mornajay rice water; he took it very well," he shouted down to her. "Now it is time for us to eat."

"Yes," she said and stood up, resolutely putting aside her turbulent thoughts for later. What was important now, dwarfing any foolish speculations about the Acharya, was that after they ate their rice they would set out for the Shan camp, and her heart beat faster with a sickening suspense as to whether they would find Cyrus there.

The Acharya did not eat his rice with them.

"How did you find the Acharya?" she asked Prasert as they seated themselves on the floor to eat. Doubtfully she regarded the bowls of food in front of her: there was the ubiquitous sticky-rice and pot of tea, but a bowl of fried prawns had been added today, which Mrs. Pollifax contemplated with enthusiasm until she realized that this modest offering had to be shared with five monks and Bonchoo. "And what made you decide to be a monk?"

"But we are novices, not monks," Prasert told her, turning to his three friends to translate this. "Me, I come here from very small, very poor village in the mountains—two hours' walk from here—and what I wish for is to become English-speaking tour guide, very important nice job! It is the abbot in my small village who send me," he explained. "Because the Acharya can teach me good English, and the Five Precepts, too."

Mrs. Pollifax picked out of the bowl her second and last prawn and molded rice into a ball to follow it. "But how did the abbot find the Acharya?"

"Ah," said Prasert, beaming at her, "he once spend three days here to learn from him and speak to him."

"How long ago?" she asked quickly.

Prasert shrugged. "This I do not know. Maybe nobody know when the Acharya come here; he is—what is word?—very secret."

Bonchoo said dryly, "And to find him it is necessary to be lost in the forest, I think."

"Yes yes," Prasert said, nodding and laughing. "That is just how my abbot find him, this holy one no longer tied to the wheel."

Mrs. Pollifax nodded. "Detached," she said, and put down her bowl of rice, conceding her lack of appetite. "But I am *very* attached to life just now and filled with a desire to find my husband. I'm anxious to leave," she told Bonchoo. "While you finish I'll tell Mornajay that we're going."

She found Mornajay no longer lying on his mat but standing up and taking a few experimental steps. He glanced up at her arrival, his face damp with sweat, and managed a weak smile; she could only imagine what this effort was costing him.

"Have to get my strength back," he said and headed for his mat where he sank down and wiped his forehead with his sleeve, no longer the immaculate Mornajay but as dusty and wrinkled as she and Bonchoo.

"I hope you'll keep in mind that you've been very ill," she told him. "We really didn't think you'd pull through, you know. You need rest."

He nodded and glanced toward the door, a sadness falling across his face so that she wondered what he was seeing; whatever it was, it had to be in his mind's eye because there was no one in the corridor. Aware of her again he said curtly, "I've no time for rest."

"I came to tell you that we're leaving."

He heard this with indifference. "That husband of yours, I suppose." He added politely, "I thank you for your help."

"You're entirely welcome," she said with equal politeness, and left him.

Bonchoo and Prasert were waiting for her at the base of the staircase to the garden, chatting amiably together in Thai. She smiled at the picture they made, Prasert in his dull orange gown, head shaven, Bonchoo wearing his absurd English-gentleman's hat that appeared even more of an anachronism in this remote jungle monastery. Prasert flashed a bright smile at her. "We go?"

"We go," she said, and turned to look up at the parapet where she had first glimpsed the Acharya. "The holy man is not to be thanked?"

"He is in meditation, please." Leading them through the stubble of the garden he suddenly stopped and made a sweeping gesture with his hand. "But he go with us, you understand? His spirit, I think, it travels everywhere, like a *nohk!*" With a vivacious laugh he turned and led them around the well and past a storage bin and toward the forest.

"Like a bird," translated Bonchoo behind her.

She did not feel the Acharya's presence at all, either as a bird or a holy one, and Prasert's allusion made her rather cross. The inscription in the Acharya's book still haunted her at one level but ever since he'd announced they would be guided to the Shan camp, after all, she had been experiencing a mixture of high anticipation and high anxiety that overrode everything else, and which felt as prickly and uncomfortable as a hair shirt; she suspected that she was having an anxiety attack. She was wondering how she had ever come to believe that Cyrus would be taken to this particular Shan camp; she was remembering now that this was based on a supposition of Nouvak's in the Akha village, but there could be other camps in other places, or he could have been taken over the mountains into Burma, and they would be too late. She had never liked the words *too late,* and today they were frightening. Her mood was not lightened when Bonchoo asked Prasert how far the camp was, and Prasert said it was only forty minutes away from them. That they had been so close all this time!

Obviously the camp was not accessible, however, for as they entered the forest again it was to encounter a labyrinth of paths. Prasert almost went out of his way to pull aside the limb of a tree or a shrub and to reveal the thread of a path going off at a tangent, and then he would turn and guide them up a different trail and down another. Only once did they encounter a real trail such as they had traveled to and from the Akha village, a trail wide enough for mules or donkeys. Crossing it she heard Bonchoo muttering in a low voice behind her.

She turned. "What?"

He gave her a wry smile. "I think Prasert has been told to take us in circles."

"That's what I think, too."

"It will be hard to find the way back, *Koon* Emily."

"Very," she said tartly, certain suspicions mounting. She wondered if, like Hansel and Gretel, she might find some means of marking their route but she soon gave up this idea; unlike Cyrus she did not possess any scraps of paper, not even one with the eye of a sardine on it; she had given away her lipstick, her square of Thai silk was wrapped around her healing foot and all that remained were the coins in her purse, and the votive. Of stones there were none, for these paths were soft with decayed wood and almost springy to the step. They were also walking uphill

again now and she could only hope that it was not a mountain
that lay ahead because her current diet of rice was not particularly fortifying. She thought wistfully of baked potatoes filled
with melting butter and sprinkled with salt and pepper; to this
she added slices of hot roast beef swimming in juices, and fresh
asparagus, and she was about to consider a dessert—strawberry
shortcake, perhaps—when she halted her fantasy, accusing herself of being just another spoiled American. She could admire
Prasert, for instance, whose very leanness spoke of wiry, coiled-
up energy, and Bonchoo, who was broad and muscular, and she
reminded herself that their energy was extracted from the very
rice that left her unsatisfied, and therefore . . .

Prasert had stopped, and so abruptly that she ran into him.
She looked up from her fantasizing and her scoldings and saw
that he stood at the crest of a hill. He pointed and she looked
down at a long strip of cleared land lying below them in the sun,
a glade in which stood a cluster of dusty palm-and-bamboo sheds
and huts in an empty compound.

"Shan camp," he said.

"Yes," she said, blinking.

At that moment a man in khaki uniform walked out of a hut
and crossed the compound and she felt a stab of fear; she'd forgotten this was a military camp. She watched the man disappear
into a hut on the right, and now she saw that a man with a rifle
was seated on a bench in the shade, and that another soldier sat
beside the door of the farthest hut, almost obscured by the deep
shadow of its roof.

Turning to Prasert she said, "Tell us how to get back to the
monastery."

He said firmly, "You do not go back."

"Not go back?" she said indignantly. "Where do we go, then,
and why *not* the monastery?"

He led them back a few steps and pointed to a tree that had
been bleached and smoothed by weather until it gleamed white,
its dead branches lifted as if in supplication, a tree that should
long since have fallen but had been held upright by the dense

growth around it. He said, "There is a trail here, do you see? It will take you south to the river where there is a boat."

"River?" she echoed.

Surprised, Bonchoo said, "You mean the Mae Kok River? We're that near to Tha Ton, then?" To Mrs. Pollifax he said, "I have been there!"

"But what's Tha Ton?"

"A small village on the Mae Kok, it's on the Thai-Burma border, and it is true, a boat can be hired there. How far?" he asked Prasert.

She wanted to ask again why they were being barred from a return to the monastery but it had already become obvious that the Acharya did not wish to see her there again, or perhaps, she thought, it was Cyrus whom he wished to avoid seeing if she was fortunate enough to have Cyrus with her. *From mama . . . on my birtday. . . .* She shook herself free of this thought and concentrated on what Prasert was saying.

"Two hours' walk, and the boat will take you—" Prasert made wild, expressive motions with one hand and smiled. "To Chiang Rai!" Turning toward the glade he added, "You must not go beyond last hut down there or you will not be in Thailand, you understand? They do not like spies here so I wish you *chohk dee* —good luck!"

With that ominous announcement he pressed his fingertips together and made a *wai,* walked down the trail and disappeared from sight.

She and Bonchoo looked at each other. "Well, Bonchoo," she said.

"Yes, *Koon* Emily," he sighed.

They edged gingerly toward the rim of the hill and crouched behind a screen of tall grass to study what lay below them. There were five buildings: a long one facing them, an open shed on their right with a small hut beside it, and two below them, the five arranged in horseshoe fashion, open to the south where a circle of bare earth suggested a landing pad.

Mrs. Pollifax, pointing, said, "For helicopters?"

Bonchoo nodded. "I think yes. For big shots from Chiang Mai, maybe."

She nodded and resumed her observations and saw—not without a sigh—that the time had come for her to repay her considerable debt to Bonchoo. If she were alone, she thought, she would have chosen to reconnoiter, to approach the camp by stealth, perhaps from the other side where she could hide behind the longest building and listen and watch for signs of a prisoner. If Cyrus was there she would have found a way to free him so that they could vanish into the forest before he was missed and she was seen. Or so she reflected, knowing the risks but knowing, too, how often inspiration arrived under pressure. Unfortunately this was impossible because of Bonchoo, who needed to explain and to vindicate himself to the Shans here, needed to describe how Jacoby had lied about him so that he would have a future again. And so since she was heavily indebted to Bonchoo, she concentrated instead on what they must do instead, which was to openly walk down the hill to the camp and trust that they wouldn't be shot by a guard before they reached it.

"I count six men now," she said to Bonchoo.

"But no Red Shirt?" he said uneasily.

"No red or yellow shirts—mercifully," she told him, but also, she was thinking, no sign of Cyrus.

Five of the men crossed the compound to the small hut on their right, leaving one on guard by the door. She said doubtfully, "I suppose we should go now, don't you? Before the other men come outside again?"

Bonchoo said gloomily, "They will come outside anyway."

"True . . . Is there a cold wind blowing down your spine, Bonchoo?"

"Very cold. I am most scared, and you?"

"Scared—very," she admitted, and thought that she had never before felt so far from home, so far from everything familiar to her.

Bonchoo said, "We have a proverb, 'The mane is proof of a real lion.' We must be very *dtoh*—very big just now." He stood and held out his hand to her. "Come," he said, "we must be real lions."

Chapter 15

In Langley, Virginia, Bishop had begun to feel that some progress was being made: a woman answering to Mrs. Pollifax's description had been seen Thursday morning at a development called Hot Springs, about an hour's drive out of Chiang Mai, and to the north of it. She'd been seen in the company of a man who was either Thai or Chinese, and who wore an odd hat. They appeared to have done some arguing but they had shared boiled eggs—this was baffling—and had then driven away in a truck.

Both the eggs and the odd hat—especially the hat—intrigued Bishop but he'd not dared to interrupt the phone call that had brought them their first news of Mrs. Pollifax. What was almost as surprising was that it was McAndrews who had unearthed this information, and entirely on his own. Carstairs had said with satisfaction, "He's shaping up."

Following this, however, the news was not as good. McAndrews had continued driving northward, and about an hour south of Chiang Rai he'd noticed a blue van abandoned at the side of the road and had stopped to inspect it. There was no way of knowing if it was the blue van into which Cyrus had been crammed, but in any case it was empty. At the police blockade outside of Chiang Rai no one had seen a truck, a man in an odd hat, Mrs. Pollifax, or for that matter a blue van.

Apparently Carstairs had been impressed enough by McAndrews' enterprise to give him a fresh assignment. "Since you're already in Chiang Rai," he'd said, "I want you to drive on to Chiang Saen now—it's not far—and look up a man named Jacoby. So far you've shared your discoveries with the Thai police but this errand is strictly hush-hush, McAndrews, you understand? Chiang Saen's a small village and it shouldn't be difficult to locate him."

"Jacoby," McAndrews repeated solemnly. "Yes, sir."

"You recall the dead man you found in the hut yesterday?"

In a burst of candor McAndrews confessed that it was the first dead person he'd ever seen and that he was not likely to forget.

"Well, the dead man's name was Ruamsak," Carstairs told him, "and he's reported to have had dealings with Jacoby. That's R-U-A-M-S-A-K," he said, spelling it for him. "There could be a clue here as to where Mr. Reed's being taken, or where his wife's heading. Find out from Jacoby who Ruamsak's enemies were, and what the hell he may know or guess about this. Jacoby's done some work for us in the past so you can mention the Department, and considering his circumstances"—Carstairs did not elaborate—"you can offer him a reasonable sum of money for any information. Fifty dollars American should do it. Got that?"

McAndrews said eagerly, "Yes, sir."

"And report back to me as soon as humanly possible."

Now they waited for that return call, but because it had been eleven at night when they'd heard from McAndrews they were faced with any number of annoying obstacles: the difficulties of his finding Jacoby in the middle of the night in a sleeping village, and even of his finding a telephone from which to call them during the night if he *should* find Jacoby.

In the meantime an imperturbable Carstairs was setting fresh inquiries in motion: he had called Holloway in Bangkok again, in an attempt to learn with whom Mornajay had been drinking his margarita at the Indiana 500 on Wednesday night. Holloway had promised to make inquiries but the man's back was all that he himself had seen of him, and he reminded Carstairs that forty-eight hours had passed and it was not likely that any of his employees would remember two men sharing a brief drink that long ago.

"Try anyway, will you?" Carstairs asked casually. "Could be a breakthrough for us."

"Sure thing."

Bishop, handling two messages from Bashir Ilariyo in the Sudan, returned to Carstairs' office to find him staring thoughtfully at their detail map of Thailand on the wall. He said, "There's got to be more that we can do, damn it, there should even be some way to stop Mornajay if he's planning to disappear . . . If Thomson feels he's heading north into the mountains—in which case he'd be somewhere in this area—" His hand swept across the northern corner of Thailand and he scowled, his voice trailing away doubtfully. With a shake of his head he returned to his desk and picked up his cup of coffee, still frowning. "Inspiration badly needed, Bishop!"

"Well, at least there's news about the coup," Bishop told him. "It seems to be stalemated. Apparently this General Lueng is hoping or expecting the rest of the main army to join with him but so far it's not happening."

Carstairs nodded absently, his thoughts elsewhere. He said abruptly, "See if you can reach Thomson again at the DEA, will you? An idea arrives, and I'd rather talk to a man I know than try contacting the DEA in Chiang Mai."

Bishop put through the call, waited for Thomson to be found, handed the phone to Carstairs and listened with interest. After an exchange of pleasantries Carstairs said, "You've notified whoever's in charge in Chiang Mai, Thomson, but I'm wondering if more could be done. They're making inquiries on the ground, so to speak?" He halted, listening, and nodded. "Following through on your guess that Mornajay's headed into the mountains, and into Burma, how about sending a couple of men in a helicopter to patrol the borders? I realize it's a small and feeble hope at best, but—what?"

He listened and made a face. "Doesn't anyone know when he'll be back? How about borrowing a helicopter?" He sighed. "Frustrating. Yes, I know you're terribly understaffed—too many budget cuts again . . . Keep me posted, will you?"

He hung up. "Damn," he said. "You heard that? Thomson had already hoped for reconnaissance but their best man, a pilot by the name of Callahan, flew off yesterday to the north on an inspection tour and they can't make radio contact with him."

"But he'd surely tune in sometime," Bishop protested.

Carstairs gave him a reproachful glance. "Not if he's on the ground and not in the air."

"Oh," said Bishop meekly.

Carstairs sighed and glanced at his watch. "Let's hope we hear soon from—" He broke off at sight of a red light flashing on the telephone and picked up the receiver. His face brightened. "It's McAndrews," he said in an aside to Bishop. "Get this on tape!"

Bishop flicked on the machine and picked up the other phone to listen. Almost at once he winced: McAndrews' voice came through absurdly loud, and he was upset again.

"Slow down," Carstairs told him sharply, "you're incoherent, I can't understand you. Have you found Jacoby?"

The voice choked. "Yes, sir—that is, no, sir."

Carstairs snapped, "Well, which, for heaven's sake?"

"Both," cried McAndrews, and blurted out, "He's dead, Mr. Carstairs, I found him dead. Somebody shot him, he must have been dead at least two days. It was awful, I mean the place reeked—"

"Steady," said Carstairs gently. "Bad luck, two bodies inside of two days . . . take your time."

"Yes, sir." McAndrews drew a deep breath and said more calmly, "It was especially awful because he couldn't have weighed more than ninety pounds and his skin was a terrible shade of green. Did you know he was an opium addict? All the equipment was there."

"Yes," Carstairs said quietly. "For nearly fifteen years, I believe. We knew."

"I see . . . well, sir—" and here a touch of pride entered McAndrews' voice. *"This* time, sir—this time I remembered to make inquiries right away. I asked around and I've a description for you of the last man seen going into his guesthouse. I mean, he was *seen.* Two days ago, in broad daylight."

"Good work, McAndrews, let's have it."

"First of all he was American, sir."

"American?"

"Yes, a well-built man, six feet tall with broad shoulders, a large pale face, long jaw, well dressed, with a head of curly gray hair. A *mop* of curly gray hair someone called it."

Across the desk Carstairs and Bishop exchanged glances. "I see," Carstairs told him smoothly. "And a very good job you've done, McAndrews. Now I want you to forget everything you've told me and go back to your computers in Bangkok. We'll take over from here."

When Carstairs hung up Bishop said grimly, "Mornajay seems to be cutting quite a swath, doesn't he!"

Carstairs scarcely heard him. "Get Thomson on the phone again and tell him our man was sighted in the north two days ago, we've a description of him from Chiang Saen."

Bishop nodded but as he walked toward the door to his office he paused beside the map of Thailand on the wall and stared at it. If Mrs. Pollifax and her companion had never passed the police blockade, he was thinking, then somewhere between Chiang Mai and Chiang Rai they had vanished from a highway that ran through the mountains and was surrounded by jungle, and because he could see no secondary roads entering that highway he had the uneasy feeling that she must have forsaken the road for the jungle, or for reasons unknown had been forced into it. He placed his finger on the general area where she had disappeared, and then he moved his finger to the village of Chiang Saen and drew a line between it and the route that Mornajay would take to enter Wen Sa's territory, and his uneasiness deepened. With a passion that surprised him he hoped that if Mrs. Pollifax had entered the jungle she was not going to encounter a man whose desperate attempt to escape had already claimed its first victim.

Chapter 16

The path wound lazily down to the Shan camp through scrub and grass, with only a few trees to screen their advance. It made for a terrifyingly exposed approach, but like a lion she would be, vowed Mrs. Pollifax, and she took the lead, keeping an eye on the guard seated by the door to the hut. He seemed oblivious to them, his foot tapping the ground as if to some cosmic music until, as they drew nearer, she saw the cord running to his ear and understood that Walkmans had arrived here, too. They were fortunate: they had actually reached the base of the hill before the guard sensed movement, turned his head and saw them. With a shout he jumped to his feet, his fellow soldiers shouted back, the door to the hut opened and by the time she and Bonchoo reached the center of the compound a circle of rifles and men brought them to a stop.

The soldiers looked more like boys than men but she could see that they took their work very seriously. She said firmly, in a loud voice, "I have come to ask if my husband is here," and she was pleased to discover that her voice did not tremble in the least.

She was stared at blankly; their only response was to press

several rifles deeper into her back, making uncomfortable inroads on her spine.

"I do not think they speak English," Bonchoo whispered. "Let me try Thai, *Koon* Emily."

She shook her head; obviously there was only one solution, and clearing her throat of dust Mrs. Pollifax shouted, "Cyrus! . . . Cyrus?"

Rifles dug more aggressively into her spine, and there were troubled, angry mutterings but from a distance, muted but unmistakably familiar, there came a shout, "Emily . . . ? My God, *Emily?*"

"Cyrus!" she gasped. Recklessly she pushed away rifles and men, broke out of the circle and ran toward the long hut with the closed door. Shouts followed her, a bullet whistled over her head and another one kicked up the dust to the left of her. She flung open the door, momentarily blinded by the darkness of the interior. "Cyrus?" she faltered.

A wonderfully familiar shape started toward her from the shadows, took several steps and then tripped over a rope that tied him to a post. *"Emily!"*

He held out his arms and she flew into them, bursting into sobs of relief as she tightly hugged the warmth of him. "Oh, Cyrus," she sobbed, "I thought—I was afraid—I thought any minute they might—"

"Not yet," he said, kissing the top of her head. "Waiting for someone who speaks English to find out who I am."

"Thank heaven they waited," she gasped. "Thank God they didn't shoot you first."

"Wouldn't find out who I am, then," he pointed out reasonably.

She laughed through her tears. "Understatement!" Flinging back her head to look into his face she said, "But are you all right, Cyrus, they didn't harm you?"

"Hell of a long walk," he said gruffly. "A little tired—and damn hungry, I can tell you." He looked down at her tenderly. "Worried terribly about you, Emily. Afraid you'd follow, afraid you wouldn't . . . the more distance we traveled the more I worried—no place for you alone in these mountains."

"But I wasn't alone," she told him. "I didn't know they waited for someone who speaks English, and you didn't know that I traveled with Bonchoo. Bonchoo's outside, Cyrus, he's been such a friend—although actually, of course, he's Ruamsak."

"He is?"

"Was," she amended, "because Ruamsak's dead."

Cyrus laughed. "Not sure I quite follow that. My God, Emily, I thought I'd never see you again, except—"

"Yes?" Her eyes adjusting to the darkness now, she could see that his face had sobered. "What is it, Cyrus?"

He shook his head. "Have to tell you, m'dear, I've thought and thought—plenty of time for *that* here—and can't see any way out of this. And now you here, too, and this Ruamsak—"

"No, *Bonchoo,*" she reminded him.

"—and that's three of us. No embassy to appeal to, no police, no one knowing where we are . . ."

The door opened and four soldiers strode in, filling the space with khaki and rifles. The word *out* was unknown but their rifles spoke for them; untying Cyrus they separated them, poked, prodded and pushed them to the door, and now it was the bright sunlight that made Mrs. Pollifax blink as she left the dark hut. Shading her eyes she looked for Bonchoo and saw him sitting despondently on the bench where the original guard had sat; he was staring gloomily at two rifles trained on him by a pair of zealous young soldiers, but at sight of Mrs. Pollifax his face brightened.

"I try to tell them why we are here but they do not speak much Thai, either." His gaze moving to Cyrus he said, "Oh—big, very big!"

Since it was to this bench they were being taken, Bonchoo moved over to make room for them. "Much bigger than last seen!" he announced.

Startled, Cyrus said, "You've seen me before?"

"Yes yes—pushed into blue van in Chiang Mai, sir."

"You've been together that long, then!"

Bonchoo started to reply but from the hill on the Burma side of the compound a voice shouted, "Hü!"

"Hü," shouted back a soldier and all of them snapped to attention as two men rode into the camp, one on horseback, one on a donkey, one of them in uniform, the other—

"Red Shirt!" gasped Mrs. Pollifax.

"Trouble," groaned Bonchoo.

"Let's hope one of them speaks English," Cyrus said fervently.

"The other is very big-shot officer," Bonchoo said. "Look, he rides a *horse.*"

"Wen Sa?" she suggested.

"Somebody high up—see his leather boots, real leather they look. No sandals for him! *Pu yai ban.*"

"Who's Wen Sa?" asked Cyrus.

"Ssh," counseled Mrs. Pollifax, and solemnly quoting Bonchoo, "not a name to be spoken loudly here."

"Then who's Red Shirt?" asked Cyrus patiently.

The officer was dismounting, the dust settling around him, his men surrounding him and one of the soldiers tethering the horse to a post. "Well," began Mrs. Pollifax, seeing that attention was still focused on the two new arrivals, "that young man in the red shirt has tried twice to kill Bonchoo, once on the road to Chiang Rai and once in the jungle, except the poisoned arrow he aimed at him in the jungle hit Mr. Mornajay instead—a man who joined us at the Akha village—which is how we spent our second night in a lost monastery with a holy man."

Cyrus gave her an appreciative glance. "Emily, you've been busy as hell," he said. "If we ever get out of this—"

Red Shirt had suddenly seen the three of them seated on the bench and even from a distance Mrs. Pollifax could see his eyes narrow in anger. He spoke to the officer, who looked at him questioningly, and Red Shirt pointed. Now the officer stared at them, too. He was small and trim, bareheaded but otherwise perfectly uniformed in khaki tunic and pants, a highly polished leather belt, leather boots and a gun in a leather holster. He wore a thin mustache across his upper lip and dark glasses over his eyes, which dismayed Mrs. Pollifax because she depended upon eyes: she spoke to a person's eyes, she estimated reactions by their eyes, and character by their expression. Beside her she could feel Bonchoo stiffen.

"Like a lion," she reminded him in a whisper.

Having examined Cyrus, Mrs. Pollifax and Bonchoo, the officer strode toward them and came to a stop in front of Bonchoo. "So you remain alive," he said in impeccable clipped English. "You appear to live a charmed life, orders were given—"

"You speak English, thank heaven," broke in Mrs. Pollifax.

"Orders were given," he continued curtly, "that you be executed for informing on us."

"But I'm not an informer!" cried Bonchoo. "You think I walk miles to come here if I am guilty? I wasn't kidnapped and brought here like *Koon* Emily's *sahmee*—" He pointed at Cyrus. "I came here to tell you I am *not* an informer."

Brows lifted skeptically over the dark glasses. Turning to Cyrus he asked, "And who are you?"

"American citizen kidnapped in Chiang Mai," he snapped, "and who are you, damn it?"

"Please—no offensive language, my ears are very delicate. I am Colonel Lu of the Shan Liberation Army." He bowed slightly and turned back to Bonchoo. "You were saying?"

"I am saying Jacoby must have told lies of me, it has to have been Jacoby who tells you such lies!"

"You deny you were selling information about our camps and supply lines?"

"I do," Bonchoo said with dignity, "and I have walked all these mountains to say this. I do not deny information but the information was *political,* it is about a coup—there is to be a coup in my country, it was about that, *only* that!"

The Colonel's brows had lifted again. "About *what?*"

"A coup—the government in Bangkok to be overthrown, and if Jacoby told you different he lies. Colonel, I have a wife and five children, how can I live in peace if your men keep trying to kill me? I ask you—"

The Colonel brushed this aside impatiently. "You can prove this?"

Bonchoo pointed to Cyrus. "I think *he* has the information I try to sell to Americans."

Cyrus looked startled and then uneasy. He said, "I really don't think—I'm sorry to say that I've not the slightest idea what he's talking about."

"Well?" said the Colonel.

Desperately Bonchoo said, "I would ask him to empty his pockets, please!"

"Very well, empty your pockets," the Colonel told Cyrus.

Cyrus began emptying his pockets. From the one he brought out coins and a roll of Thai money, and from the other he brought out a used roll of film, a pencil, a pen and a wide lacquer-and-yarn bracelet.

"There," cried Bonchoo, "the *phyot* arm-ring, see? That's it, that's it!"

"That?" said the Colonel skeptically.

"Let me show you!" Bonchoo seized the arm-ring, his hand moving toward his pocket; abruptly he stopped. "If I may borrow a knife?"

Mrs. Pollifax breathed a sigh of relief; he had come very close to drawing out his Shan murder knife, which would have been tactless, to say the least. The Colonel spoke to his men, rifles were lifted, a knife produced and then rifles lowered to again point at the three of them.

Gripping the knife Bonchoo cut away the woven yarn, exposing and then unfolding the rolled-up tube of paper. Cyrus stared at it in astonishment. "Good God, *that's* what they were after? Thought it one of Emily's souvenirs!"

Bonchoo held out the letter. "It's written in Vietnamese, Colonel, written by a Thai general named Lueng, and just as I tell you, it is about a coup."

"I will see for myself, I know some Vietnamese," the Colonel said coldly. He removed his dark glasses, tucked them into a pocket of his tunic and brought out a pair of reading glasses. Scanning the letter he said, "But this is about a coup!"

"Yes yes," Bonchoo said eagerly.

The Colonel, reading it more carefully, smiled. "And with such tact—and yes, a charming touch of acid—the officer in Laos refuses to help this Lueng with his coup. Oh, very good! He ends with, 'Revolution will come by itself when the workers and the peasants demand to be heard.' " He looked up from the letter to say crisply, "The coup began yesterday morning in Bangkok."

"Already?"

"Yes. This is dangerous information but it is late, very late." He handed it back to Bonchoo. "It is amusing to see but it is of no interest to us, we are Shan fighting for our liberation from the Burmans." He shrugged. "It may, however, be of interest to the Americans—take it back."

Bonchoo said, "What I would most like to take back is my name as honest teak smuggler."

"Take that, too," the Colonel said, and turned to speak to Red Shirt. With a nod to Bonchoo he said, "I have told Phibul here that all orders for you to be killed are now canceled and that Jacoby made a very grave mistake."

Bonchoo made a *wai*. "I am most grateful."

"And now can we go, please?" asked Mrs. Pollifax eagerly.

His gaze rested on her thoughtfully. "You have certainly come a long way. One wonders how you found us."

"Yes."

"And certainly it is an inconvenience to have you here."

Cyrus said calmly, "Then we'll be delighted to relieve you of our presence, and since you've already established Mr. Bonchoo's innocence and assured him—"

The Colonel interrupted. "I see that you don't perfectly understand. For myself I toy with the attractions of letting you go, since we break camp this afternoon and will no longer be in this area should you carelessly speak of us being here. However, this is impossible."

"Why?" asked Mrs. Pollifax.

"Because we expect a helicopter shortly with a very high-level person to join us who might not look so kindly on such an act of benevolence. I have met this man, he is not a Buddhist and I might add that he lacks a playful attitude. It will be up to him to decide."

"Decide what?" asked Cyrus.

He shrugged. "Whether you will be free to go. My own interest is in fighting a war but his interests are different, very different."

"And what if he says not?" demanded Cyrus.

He looked surprised. "Why, then, you would be killed and buried here, of course."

"Killed!" cried Mrs. Pollifax. "But what have we done?"

"It's not what you've done, it's what you've seen," he said stiffly, and walked away.

"But what have we seen?" she cried after him in protest.

Watching him go, Bonchoo said bitterly, "To me he gives with one hand and takes away with the other. Of what use to clear my name if instead of the *naklengs* killing me somebody else does?"

"But what have we seen?" repeated Mrs. Pollifax. "How can he speak of killing like that?"

"Steady, m'dear," Cyrus said, reaching for her hand and holding it. "It's probably what I've seen and you've not had time to notice. Behind us, in that long open shed."

She turned her head to see that under the shed's thatch roof stood row upon row of cloth sacks, perhaps a hundred of them, neatly packaged like bags of flour. "Oh," she faltered. "Opium?"

"Don't look," Bonchoo pleaded after he, too, had looked.

"Is it opium?" she demanded of him.

He sighed. "It would be morphine, *Koon* Emily, there must be their refinery very near, maybe over that hill. In the refinery they cook opium down into morphine and dry it in the sun, which makes it very small and light to carry. Those bags must be waiting for pack animals to carry them down from the mountains."

She said indignantly, "Well, their morphine would surely be long-since gone by the time we reached Chiang Mai!" She glared at the young man who was guarding them. "If we're going to be killed for *that*—"

"Could be other reasons," Cyrus suggested. "Know what you're thinking, m'dear, but I've not a single match with me, have you?" When she only shook her head he said quietly, "It's your great talent for optimism that we need very much just now."

"Optimism," she repeated and was silent, wondering where it had gone. She was very tired, of course, but she realized that after hearing Colonel Lu's announcement she felt utterly drained of optimism and rather frightened. It was true that she had pursued Cyrus with a great deal of optimism and with a one-track mind as well, but she had not looked beyond the joy of finding him. Cyrus had taken a much shrewder measure of their situation than she: he had seen how cheap human life could be in this world of smugglers, warlords and drug merchants, where even their being American was a strike against them. She supposed that she had entertained too many assumptions and expectations: she had assumed that they could leave, and then she had learned that it was not to be that simple, that a stranger would arrive in a helicopter to decide their fate, and this was a shock to her expectations.

She did not speak; they were each of them silent, absorbed by the unpleasant news that they might not survive this day. Several feet away from her their guard watched them closely and with obvious curiosity: she noticed that each small movement, each gesture was observed and cataloged as if he'd never seen Americans before, but his eyes held no hostility. She felt that under other circumstances he would want to ask many questions of them: whether Americans knew about the Shan people, whether all Americans wore shoes of leather, as Cyrus did—his gaze went to them frequently—and what had brought them here, but his rifle remained steadily pointed at them and his eyes alert; he was young and he was conscientious and she had no doubt that he would shoot them if they made any reckless moves. Beyond him three of the soldiers had begun dismantling the hut in which she'd found Cyrus. Prefabricated housing had come early to the jungle, she thought, watching them detach each wall of woven bamboo from its post and roll it up like a carpet. Under a tree the Colonel had set up a radio and was speaking into it, with glances at the sky and an air of expectation. To the right of him a soldier squatted on the ground with an opened betal box. She watched him place a leaf in the palm of his hand and delicately extract powders from his box which he mixed on the leaf; when this had been done he placed the leaf in his mouth and began to chew slowly, methodically and with much pleasure, occasionally spitting a stream of red to the earth.

She said at last, "Who do you suppose this person is that we're waiting for, this man who decides whether we live or—or—"

"Or die," Cyrus said gently. "Say it, m'dear, get the word out."

"All right—die," she said, naming it.

His hand tightened in hers. "We've had a good run for it, you know, a damn good one, Emily."

She admitted this. "Except that to find you alive, Cyrus, has raised the most abominable expectations of our having a few more years together . . . for two days now I've wondered how I ever enjoyed life without you."

He smiled. "Then it's not so bad if we die together, is it?"

She smiled back at him. "Thank you for that, I think it's a lovely attitude."

"Afraid of death?"

She shook her head. "It's hovered very close a number of times, you know. No I'm not afraid but I admit to some—well, adjustment that it could happen today—so abruptly—in the next hour or so. I did hope to see our house again, and the garden, and another spring, and—oh I *must* be tired, Cyrus, I'm sorry!"

"Can't think why you'd be tired," he said with a smile and held her close, comforting the disappointed child in her until she remembered Bonchoo and drew away, smiled at Cyrus gratefully and turned to Bonchoo.

He was carefully not watching them. "Bonchoo?" she said.

"No, I am not afraid either, *Koon* Emily," he said with dignity. "A Buddhist accepts, and I will die today or not die today, and if I do—well, that is my karma. My regret is that I killed the Shan and drank rice wine with the Akhas, for wine is forbidden to a good Buddhist. In my next life this will be much against me."

"Nonsense," Cyrus said indignantly, "I'll intervene for you, I'll make very clear that any merit you lost has been bloody-well gained back by now."

"You think so?" He thought about this. "But I feel much out of reach of the *phi*-spirit who protects me in my village; I have walked too far." Sadly he shook his head. "My wish now is that I had asked the holy man this morning to bless an amulet for me."

"You mentioned a holy man," Cyrus said. "Having never met a holy man, what's he like?"

Mrs. Pollifax remained silent. It was Bonchoo who described him as a man who had awakened to his Buddha-nature, and without ego lived in a forgotten temple in the jungle, gathering wisdom through meditation.

"And did you think him a holy man, too?" Cyrus asked her.

Mrs. Pollifax hesitated, unsure of herself, wanting to speak of the inscription in his book that puzzled her, but telling herself there was no proof of her bizarre suspicions, and that to speak of them in front of Bonchoo would be unkind to the Acharya. She said slowly, "He refused us help at first, which made me very angry at the time, but for reasons that I think I understand now. Yes, there was something about him, something quite—quite rare," she said, aware of her ineptness.

Bonchoo nodded. "An amulet from him would have protected us," he said, and with a glance at her wristwatch he added wistfully, "it is four o'clock? My children would be coming home from school now in my village, and my mother-in-law would be waking from her nap, and my wife back from the market." He sighed and then went on, his voice becoming more cheerful. "Because she is very smart, my wife, she would have received good money for the eggs she sold. And in a few hours, by seven o'clock, there would be a good dinner. You have not had proper

Thai dinner," he told Mrs. Pollifax firmly. "We would give you *Tom-yum*—good hot soup—and *Gaeng ped,* which is curry with coconut milk, and *Khai palo* or *Horn-muk*—steamed fish—and melons very sweet and juicy."

"You're making my mouth water," Cyrus told him. "What are the names of your children?"

"You wish to know?" he said, pleased. "I have five. The two girl-children are Amporn and Panngham, the three boys are Praphas, Charoon and Pote."

"And your wife?" asked Mrs. Pollifax.

"She is called Mi-mi."

Beside her Cyrus suddenly stiffened. "Listen—do you hear it, too?"

"The helicopter?" asked Mrs. Pollifax, and learned all over again that the cessation of waiting could be as traumatic as the waiting itself. The soldiers had also heard it and were gathering next to the Colonel under his tree, their guard with them, so that Mrs. Pollifax, pointing to him, said, "Do you think we could make a run for it now?"

This drew a smile from Bonchoo. "They too can run, *Koon* Emily, and they have guns."

"Sensible man," said Cyrus. "Ah—there it is!"

The helicopter hovered, looking a mere toy in the great blue sky, an impertinent eagle waiting to pounce. It remained poised above the compound and then began its vertical descent, the tops of trees bending under the assault of its backwash, its roto-blades sending up clouds of dust as it touched the ground. The door was lifted away, a man tossed two duffel bags to the turf and then eased himself to the earth. Picking up the duffel bags he ducked to one side, and once he was clear the helicopter lifted and zig-zagged off to the east.

Mrs. Pollifax gasped, "Cyrus—he looks American!"

Bonchoo said, "Certainly he is not Thai or Chinese—English?"

"I wonder: good or bad," murmured Cyrus.

"But American—*here?*" she said.

Colonel Lu did not go forward to meet the man but waited for him beside the tree. The man strode toward him, lean and confident and looking as he'd just been snatched from the streets of Bangkok in his white shirt and tie, well-cut jacket and chino slacks. As he drew closer and Mrs. Pollifax could see his face she was surprised by his attractiveness: it was not a strong face but it was certainly a handsome one, boyish in spite of the curly black hair threaded with gray, and definitely he looked American. There was a rakish quality about him and she saw lines of dissipation in his face, but his deep tan enhanced the pale blue eyes and were a distraction from the mouth and chin, which were weak. She thought he looked a man who would be long on charm and that he would want and need to test that charm frequently on women.

And this was the man who was to decide their fates; she did not feel hopeful, not with that mouth and chin.

Colonel Lu bowed, making a formal *wai*. "Mr. Chollee, is it not?" he said. "Welcome, it has been many years since we met."

The man stopped, his eyes narrowing as he saw the three of them seated on the bench. "Who are those people?" he demanded. "Where did they come from, what the hell are they doing here?"

"It has been a private matter," the Colonel said courteously.

"Nothing's private here, who are they? What I don't need are a pair of tourists and a Thai, damn it, what are they doing here, how did they find the camp?" His voice was almost petulant, high-pitched and urgent.

Cyrus called out to him angrily, "Didn't *find* the camp, I was kidnapped and brought here—no choice at all—and this is my wife and this is a friend and who the devil are *you?*"

"You see?" said Mr. Chollee to the Colonel. "Americans are like this—curious and demanding. *And they have seen me.*"

"Yes, they have seen you."

"We let them go and they talk, which doesn't fit into my plans at all."

Colonel Lu shrugged. "It's entirely in your hands, of course."

"Then kill them," the man said dismissingly. "Kill them now."

"Oh," gasped Mrs. Pollifax.

"Look here," began Cyrus.

"Shut up," Chollee told him. "Kill them, Lu."

The Colonel shook his head. "This I will not do, Mr. Chollee. I fight a war, and to kill in war is one matter. We Shan did not hesitate to kill the Japanese in World War Two when they overran our country, but to kill without reason is to lose great merit. It is due to a mistake of my men that they are here at all. This I will have nothing to do with."

"You Buddhists," Chollee said irritably. "All right, I'll kill them myself but I hope you're not too squeamish to get your men digging some graves."

"They will dig three graves for you," the Colonel said stiffly, "but not kill for you. If Americans wish to kill Americans it is not my business." He walked away and his men followed, looking back with curious glances.

"Oh how dare you," whispered Mrs. Pollifax.

He laughed. "Easily! Stand up, now. Line up in a row."

So it's really going to happen—like an execution, she thought, *a hasty one at that,* and she reached for Cyrus' hand. A certain calm surprised and dignified her as she took her place between Bonchoo and Cyrus. The Colonel had withdrawn but she could hear the sound of shovels digging and the soft thud of earth as graves began to be hollowed out of the ground. The sun shone on palms and bamboo and a faint breeze sent dust motes dancing. She held Cyrus' hand, trembling only a little.

In the forest a bird cried out shrilly.

She heard the click of his safety catch released.

He lifted his revolver and aimed it.

In one second now, she thought . . . *in just one second . . .* She closed her eyes.

"Drop it, Charlie!" shouted a voice from the trees behind them. "Drop your gun, I've got you covered!"

She opened her eyes. She caught a glimpse of Charlie's face, saw it register shock and incredulity, and then she turned with

Cyrus and Bonchoo to see the man who came limping into the compound.

It was Mornajay, deathly pale but upright, his revolver leveled at their executioner.

Chapter 17

"You!" cried Charlie, his face turned into a mask of hate and fury. "How did you know, how did you get here, damn it, how—was it Jacoby?"

Mornajay said scornfully, "That friend of yours you hooked on opium? No, it wasn't Jacoby."

"Then who—"

"Chin-Ling," he said.

Charlie's eyes blazed. "You're lying, I don't believe you, she'd never—"

"You broke too many promises to her," Mornajay said evenly. "She told me you're on the run, she gave me longitude, latitude and date, Charlie. I've come to take you back."

"Back!" Charlie laughed. "On one of your bloody rescue missions again? Well, my answer to that is damn you and damn you again."

"Yes, you've certainly tried hard enough to do that," said Mornajay. "Drop your gun, Charlie, or I'll shoot it out of your hand."

"You wouldn't dare," he sneered. "Look at you; if I threw a pebble at you you'd fall over."

"Don't try me, Charlie."

"Thank God where I'm going you'll never find me again!"

"You're not going anywhere, Charlie."

"Look out!" cried Cyrus as Charlie's hand moved.

Two guns fired simultaneously, the sound of them reverberating among the hills and returning to them before the echo died away. Dust rose from the impact of a body hitting the ground. In the jungle a mynah bird scolded noisily and subsided. The trees themselves seemed to sigh; the silence after the moment of violence was almost voluptuously complete and silken.

Mornajay stood dazed, staring at the fallen Charlie. He whispered, "Oh my God," and swayed on his feet.

"There's blood on your sleeve," Mrs. Pollifax told him, and she went to him.

"Only grazed me," he said impatiently, and noticing her for the first time, "Mrs. Pollifax again, isn't it? Need a bit of help," he said with a twisted smile. "There's a backpack behind the tree over there—over where the stretcher is." He pointed. "Somebody get it."

"You persuaded the monks to bring you!"

"Only way—that or crawl," he said with that same unreal grimace of a smile. His gaze went to the man sprawled on the ground and she saw tears in his eyes. "Help me over to him, will you?"

Bonchoo said quickly, "I'll get the backpack."

Leaning on Mrs. Pollifax, Mornajay walked unsteadily to the dead man and stood looking down at him. "Never could shoot straight," he said sadly, and sank to his knees beside him.

"You know him," said Mrs. Pollifax, speaking the obvious.

Mornajay reached out a trembling hand and tenderly closed the wide-open staring dead eyes. He said bitterly, "He died still hating, still trying to destroy me." His voice broke. "He's right, you know, I should have stopped rescuing him long ago. The forged checks, stolen money, promises broken, people hurt, but to learn—" He drew a long, shuddering sigh. "To learn—find out —be told *this* is what he'd come to!"

"Who is he?" she asked.

"My brother," he said in a broken voice. "My family."

She looked away, moved by the longing she heard behind that word *family,* the cry of a lonely man struggling to be loved. She tried to remember the imperious Mornajay of the Akha village, and she discovered that she wanted him back. She could only wait silently and as unobtrusively as possible while he struggled for control; she wasn't sure that any of them existed for him at this moment.

He said at last, turning away, "I'll take him back with me, I can't leave him here . . . a grave so far from everything he knows—knew—" He shook his head. "It seems there's nothing left for me to rescue now except the name of Mornajay . . ."

"I suppose that's important," she said, helping him to his feet.

He gave her a glance so sharp that she saw the other man behind the grief, the man accustomed to authority, privacy, success: the Mornajay she'd met earlier was surfacing at last, and she was relieved.

"In some circles," he said dryly, "it is a name that's known for its integrity."

"Bonchoo's brought your backpack," she pointed out.

He nodded. "The Shans, they've gone?"

Bonchoo shook his head. "They're up on the hill watching."

"Then help me to that rock," said Mornajay sharply. "There's not much time, we've got to work fast. There's a radio in the backpack—you," he said to Cyrus. "You must be the husband. You look intelligent—"

"Moderately, yes," said Cyrus with a twinkle in his eye.

"Set up the radio for me, will you? I've not much strength, damn it. And you—Bonchoo, isn't it? In the backpack you'll find a small tin of lighter fluid, matches and a newspaper."

I missed seeing THOSE, thought Mrs. Pollifax.

"Crumple the newspapers, soak them in the fluid and shove them into those bags of morphine for burning."

"Wonderful—I'll help," said Mrs. Pollifax, and feeling amused now by his return to Mornajay-normalcy she said, "Are you going to give us time soon to thank you for saving our lives?"

"No need to be maudlin. Anyway," he added with an embarrassed smile, "I seem to recall that you contributed to mine." He sank down on the rock and mopped his forehead. He looked ghastly; she wanted to ask him a dozen questions, wanted to ask how on earth he hoped to take back his brother's body when he could scarcely walk himself, she wanted to ask who he was, and how he'd persuaded the novices to bring him here, and who Chin-Ling was, and how he happened to know the name of Jacoby, and what he hoped for from the radio.

Instead, silently, she helped Bonchoo open the tin of lighting fluid, find the matches and crumple the paper while Cyrus lifted the radio out of Mornajay's backpack and handed it up to him on the rock. Crackling sounds ensued, Mornajay reset dials and adjusted volume.

When he spoke he surprised her. "Callahan?" he called crisply. "This is M, are you hearing me?"

So he'd not come alone . . . She exchanged glances with Bonchoo and they stopped working to frankly listen. After a cloud of static a voice answered. "Receiving you, M, you okay?"

"One casualty—X is dead." His voice faltered and then steadied. "Camp's about five miles farther south than anticipated. How soon can you be here?"

"Trouble?"

"Could be."

"Ten minutes. Can you give precise bearings?"

Mornajay smiled faintly. "No need, there's going to be one hell of a bonfire here shortly that will guide you in, Callahan. Look for the smoke."

"Reading you, M . . . you okay?"

"A-okay," said Mornajay grimly, and handing the radio back to Cyrus he returned the gun to his lap.

"Drug Enforcement Agency?" asked Cyrus with a lift of his eyebrows.

"I don't think introductions are necessary," Mornajay said with his usual curtness. "I don't know who you are and I don't want to, although how a couple of tourists got here is beyond me, and who I am doesn't matter in the slightest."

"Is it a plane coming?" asked Mrs. Pollifax, wanting to be sure.

"Helicopter. Sorry there'll be no room for you," he said gruffly, "which is why I suggest that as soon as you light that fire you get the hell out of here, and for heaven's sake stay hidden while you light it. The only thing I can do for you is make certain you're not implicated in the burning of this stuff—that fire is going to cost somebody close to a million dollars. If Wen Sa is on the hill watching—"

"Wen Sa?" gasped Bonchoo.

Mornajay said dryly, "He may have called himself something else but the man I saw here in uniform earlier answers to all the descriptions known of Wen Sa."

Bonchoo shivered. "Yai—I have met Wen Sa?"

"Leave now. You've time to reach Tha Ton before dark, Prasert told me you'd been shown the trail."

Bonchoo nodded.

"What about you?" asked Cyrus. "I counted eight Shans and you can't hold them even for ten minutes if they rush you."

"No?" Again Mornajay smiled that twisted smile. "My gun will hold them off—there's Charlie's gun too—and Callahan is on his way." He checked his watch.

"Eight against one," Cyrus said doubtfully. "I think we ought to stay until Callahan arrives."

Mornajay laughed. "Light the fire, will you? What could you do without guns except get in the way? If I die, I die . . . the one thing I can't do, damn it, is hobble over there and light that fire."

"We're doing it now," called Mrs. Pollifax, with a nod to Bonchoo, and he struck the first match.

"Good—and then for God's sake leave before they see any smoke. Move it!"

Mrs. Pollifax lit the last match, saw it ignite the last sheet of crumpled paper and reached for her purse.

"Emily? Bonchoo?" said Cyrus, waiting.

"For this I do not need to be begged," said Bonchoo, and he ran with Mrs. Pollifax to join Cyrus, who turned and led them up the hill at a brisk pace.

When they reached the crest they stopped for a second to catch their breath and look back. Mornajay made a lonely figure seated in the center of the compound, the gun in his hand, the backpack on his lap. Beyond him smoke drifted lazily up from the pile of dried opium, scarcely discernible as yet, and then a tongue of flame ran up one side, and then another . . .

Bonchoo said, "A strange man—a little mad, I think, and *very* rude, but—we did not die today, *Koon* Emily—and we return with your *sahmee* after all!"

Chapter 18

Some eighteen hours later, on Sunday afternoon, Cyrus, Mrs. Pollifax and Bonchoo limped into the airport at Chiang Rai, jaded, considerably disheveled and near to exhaustion. It had been Bonchoo who guided them to the village of Tha Ton, Bonchoo who found them food and a place to sleep for the night and Bonchoo who bargained with the owner of a long-tailed boat with a stripped-down V-8 engine, which earned them—as if there had not been enough excitement, thought Mrs. Pollifax—a six-hour race downriver the next morning through rapids, past ominous boulders, through a narrow gorge and finally to Chiang Rai.

It was also Bonchoo who insisted on escorting them to the airport for the plane to Bangkok.

"But you'll miss your bus home to Chiang Saen," she protested again, when Cyrus went off to buy their tickets.

He said gravely, "I do this because I would much better like to invite you to my village to rest, but I do not think it so restful there, so like first-class guide I escort you."

Cyrus, joining them again, grinned. "Not restful because of Charoon, Praphas, Pote, Amporn and Panngham?"

"You have good memory," Bonchoo said, smiling up at him.

"They would be all excitement to meet you, yes, but it is not like hotel, and you are both—"

"Older peoples?" suggested Cyrus with a twinkle.

"Very *tired* peoples," Bonchoo said with a reproachful glance.

"How about a raincheck?" asked Mrs. Pollifax.

"Raincheck?" he said, puzzled.

"She means we could visit you later, after we've convalesced," said Cyrus. "Before we leave your country for home. What about it, Emily?"

"Oh I'd love that," she said warmly. "To see you again—to meet your family—"

Bonchoo's eyes brightened. "Then it is not goodbye after all, *Koon* Emily!"

"Not goodbye, no. Oh, and Bonchoo—" With a smile at Cyrus she reached into her purse and brought out the Buddhist votive. "Ruamsak may be dead," she told him gravely, "but he delivered all the information before he was—er—murdered with a Shan knife, and so this was to be given to you—to Ruamsak—for services rendered."

He accepted it graciously. "A very pretty votive—I thank you."

"Not votive," said Cyrus. "Tell him, m'dear."

"Like your *phyot* arm-band it's in disguise," she told him eagerly. "It's a cube of gold."

"Gold?" he gasped. *"G-gold?"* he stammered, his eyes shining. "Yai! my wife can have a sewing machine at last, and I—maybe now I open a shop in Chiang Saen and not smuggle teak anymore!" He beamed at them happily. "It is a world of wonders, is it not? filled with *phi*-spirits and ghosts and *nagas* that have surrounded us all, and who would have thought we would live through it to see the Chiang Rai airport! You have good spirits looking after you!"

"Think so?" Cyrus said, amused.

"Oh yes, and we are most fortunate of peoples, for we have survived Wen Sa!"

She said teasingly, "A tale to be told in your village?"

"With many additions," he assured her gravely. "A *farang* of giant size carrying tins of sardines, rescued from the evil ones by a woman magician who is surely a spirit herself—"

"That's how the story will go?"

"Of course," he said, grinning.

She smiled back at him, suddenly recalling her first impressions and her doubts of him, and remembering how patient he had been with her, and how loyal. Certain vignettes tugged at her memory: of Bonchoo merrily smoking a cheroot in the Akha village; of Apha's joy at being given a tube of lipstick, a mirror, a cluster of safety pins; of an outraged American who had been mistaken for Cyrus. She thought of Colonel Lu, and of Mornajay's strange pilgrimage, but most of all she remembered a temple in the jungle with three dreaming Buddhas and a holy man.

"It's goodbye then for only a little while," she said, and to her surprise she was hugged by Bonchoo.

"Yes—you come soon, but first to Bangkok."

"To sleep," she said, nodding.

"For at least two days," Cyrus added with a grin and they headed out to the plane waiting on the tarmac.

But Mrs. Pollifax had no intention of sleeping late the next day, there was still something important to be done, and the next morning, once again at the Oriental Hotel, she was awake by seven. She lay quietly for a moment, savoring the miracle of Cyrus asleep beside her, and turned her head to be sure—yes, he was still there, he was real—and then she carefully slid out of bed to avoid waking him. From the window she could look down on the river. Somewhere below lay the terrace, and as she dressed she remembered the day an eternity ago when she had pictured them back here in a matter of hours to once again watch the barges and pleasure boats passing on the river. And now they were here, five days late and considerably wiser, but they were here.

How strange life can be, she thought, and lifting the guidebook from Cyrus' suitcase she sat down, opened it, ran her fingers down the index and turned to a certain page. She had a choice, she noted, but she copied out only one of the addresses, the one most accessible at this hour of the day. Scrawling a note for Cyrus—BACK SOON—she propped it on the bureau and tiptoed out of the room.

Descending in the elevator she did not turn to the right and head for the terrace but proceeded through the glass doors to the taxi stand. The elegantly uniformed concierge summoned a cab for her, she gave the address—95 Wireless Road—and asked that the driver be instructed to wait for her there.

It was not a long drive. Once at her destination she stepped out of the cab to enter the gardens and grounds of the U.S. Embassy and to be met at once by the fragrance of flowers and of freshly cut grass. She paused briefly to admire jasmine and bougainvillea, but already she had caught a glimpse of what she had come to see and now she moved impatiently toward it.

It was a bronze statue, prominently displayed near the path and encircled by a bed of bright flowers. As she drew close it seemed to tower over her—as three Buddhas had once towered over her, she remembered. Reaching it she politely read the plaque that identified the figure as John Lloyd Matthews and then she looked up into the face. But bronze was very different from flesh, she thought, and she stood under it for several minutes, frowning and in doubt, for the sculptor had posed the man gazing off into the horizon and he looked bloodless and official. The features vaguely matched but she reflected dryly that the head of the man in bronze was not shaven. Still in doubt she stepped around a rose bush and moved to the side. Reaching the profile she gasped. At once—with a jarring abruptness—she was swept back in time to the parapet of a crumbling temple in the mountains where she had last seen this profile etched against a moonlit sky, calm and serene in deep meditation.

There was no longer any doubt: she was staring at the Acharya.

How very strange, she thought, and yet . . . and yet . . . how very right, somehow.

Dimly she became aware that a man had stopped beside her to look at both her and the statue. He spoke now, and she turned to look at him: a young man carrying a briefcase, obviously headed for the Embassy. Gazing at the statue he said, "He was a great man, you know—name of John Lloyd Matthews."

"Yes," she said. "Did you know him?"

He shook his head. "I was assigned here too late to know him, unfortunately, but I saw him—just once—a few days before he left for Chiang Mai and disappeared." He shivered. "If he was murdered I hope he died quickly."

Mrs. Pollifax thought about this and smiled. "To the things of the world I'm sure that he died quickly—very quickly."

"A pity what happened to him," he went on, scarcely heeding her oblique words. "It seems such a waste, he changed so many things in Thailand for the better, you know."

"Perhaps Thailand changed many things in him, too," she said softly. "For the better," she added with a smile, and with a polite nod she returned to her waiting taxi to go back and tell Cyrus of her discovery: that among the people to whom they owed their lives there could now be added the name of his old friend Joker Matthews.

On Wednesday morning Carstairs said to Bishop, "By the way, Mornajay's back in his office this morning."

Bishop's jaw dropped. "What, no scandal, no investigation, no early retirement? I must say that's mysterious!"

"Well, this *is* the CIA," Carstairs pointed out. "Home of mysteries, digressions, covert and overt coverups, et cetera et cetera et cetera. I hear that he looks ghastly, he's apparently been quite ill."

"Aren't you curious?" asked Bishop.

Carstairs smiled, picked up his cup of coffee and leaned back in his chair. "Bishop," he said, "I am very curious. I would like *very* much to know what Mornajay was up to, and where he's been and why he killed Jacoby—which I'm certain he did . . . I would also like very much to know why Mrs. Pollifax was so deliberately evasive in her phone call to us as to where the hell she and Cyrus had been for five days. But since they're off viewing temples now, and inaccessible, and since Mornajay has been restored to us, one must be philosophic . . . What's important is that the coup failed in Bangkok, Mrs. Pollifax and Cyrus are safe and the evidence against Lueng on its way to us, Mornajay is back at his desk and we are all of us—thank God—in our appointed places again."

"Amen," said Bishop with feeling. "I take it we can now dispense with our Thailand-watching, after its occupying us for one hell of a long week?"

"Consider it back in the hands of the DEA now," said Carstairs cheerfully. "Who incidentally reported a raid in northern Thailand last weekend, and nine hundred pounds of dried opium burned to an ash."

Bishop chuckled. "Maybe that's where Mrs. Pollifax was— maybe Emily lit the fire."

Carstairs gave him a pitying glance. "Your imagination certainly knows no limits, Bishop. Curb it and get back to those reports on the Sudan, will you?"

"Yes, sir," Bishop said and retreated to his office to begin another day's work.